Endless Time

A Novel

ENDLESS TIME

A Novel

DANIEL HILL ZAFREN

Published by Time Treasures Books, Goose Creek, South Carolina
www.timetreasuresbooks.com

ISBN: 978-0-9833042-8-9

Printed in the United States of America

Cover and interior by Susan Newman Design Inc.

MYSTERY OF THE MARSH

Moonlight flickers on the depths of the marsh,
 Eery winds animate vegetation in strange ways;
The sounds coming from within are mellow and harsh,
 Repetitive cycles away from view over countless days.

One does not venture into the marsh without fears,
 Unexplained disappearances told in countless stories;
Prompting strong emotions and boundless tears,
 Leading to further apprehension and grave worries.

Many say the marsh is a very special evil place,
 To be avoided by all at any cost;
For people to vanish within without a trace,
 Once in its grasp all is lost.

The marsh is real and beckons to all,
Be wise and do not answer its call!

Daniel Hill Zafren

ONE

"What are you going to do when you retire?" Whenever Grady Oslow was asked this question or a variation of it, there could be no complete or truthful answer. His response would be unclear and general, such as, "A little of this and a little of that. Maybe some traveling, or even writing and painting." He knew exactly what he was going to do, and he had known it for a long time. It was not anything that could be easily explained or understood. In fact, it was not something that should be stated or even alluded to. Whenever he had the perfect place to carry it out at and the appropriate people to assist him, it was only then a matter of waiting for that retirement.

Grady had been preparing for it most of his working years. It would take a good deal of money, at least initially. Later, rewards would be great both monetarily and in satisfaction. In the mean time, it entailed large personal sacrifices to save money. In his obscure research job in the Parliamentarian's Office in the Capitol in Washington, D.C. he was little noticed and led the most frugal of life styles. He lived for over thirty years in a rental two room apartment in an old building on Capitol Hill. He had no automobile and walked to and from work. He never took an extended vacation that required anything but minimal expenses. His taste in food, clothes, and entertainment was simple if not downright cheap. He had never married or even dated, and while he would have liked female companionship at times, it paled in the light of his overall mission. A scheme unfulfilled is no scheme at all.

Since he had borrowing privileges from the Library of Congress, he was a fastidious reader. His interests were far-reaching, and he especially enjoyed learning about obscure subjects and unusual experiences. He kept his body in shape with long walks through the Capitol grounds, and he studied all about plants in the Arboretum that was also on the Capitol grounds.

Being in the background of the center of important actions and activities of elected officials, lobbyists, and other influence-driven people wanting to partake in the movement of government, Grady discovered early on that if he fine-tuned listening he could hear things that perhaps no one else could or should hear. Then, all he had to do was to piece together the snippets and evolve with the planning proposed or suggested. The birth of the idea came early on in his working days when he innocently overheard two senators talking in a corner of the Capitol hallway. After a critical discussion of an official's actions, one whispered to the other, "There should be some sophisticated and foolproof way to eliminate those who threaten the true values of the country." The other senator nodded in agreement.

That may have been the first time his mind was introduced to such a radical idea, but it was not the last. Over the years, Grady had heard similar expressions involving the public sector, and it was easy to extend the concept to the business world and to personal situations. A particular need giving rise to a special business. It was not up to him to judge whether it was a legitimate need or even moral in nature. The recurring thought was that such a specialized need would bring a fortune his way. His sacrifices would bring rewards well beyond his wildest dreams.

Grady had anticipated that it would be more difficult to find just the right people to participate in such a venture with him than to find a place for its operation. Yet, just the right people were easy to line up. It might be said they fell right in his lap. A towering black man, Gideon Humple, nicknamed Cuba because that is where he was born and who could have been a football player but never played the sport and never went to college, lived in an apartment with his wife, Hilda, across the hall from his apartment. Cuba was easily six foot three inches tall and probably tipped the scale in the 300 pound range. Hilda was also a large person and nearly as muscular as Cuba. The two made an imposing pair and easily shadowed over Grady's five foot seven inch frame.

Cuba and Hilda had been his neighbors since he had been in the building. They were hardly ever there, however. Cuba was a head chef and Hilda a pastry chef. They worked on the cruise lines that departed from Baltimore during the year except for the summers when they worked together in some of the mountain resorts. Any days between chef jobs they spent in the Washington apartment. Over the years, a close friendship developed, and whenever they were home there were mutual visits with interesting conversation and lots of laughter. The cooking folks had seen a lot of places and Grady had rubbed elbows with many politicians. Both experiences prompted detailed and often humorous stories. The friendship grew even tighter when, as they had always wanted but could not do so because they were away so much, Cuba and Hilda adopted a pair of kittens when Grady offered to care for them in their absence. The cats were friendly and entertaining, and Grady would relate many of their antics to the Humples when they returned from a job. Just as Grady had no family, Cuba and Hilda had no relatives. Once Grady alluded to the prospects of his future and the pair working for him, they trusted him and were interested. Grady would at times elaborate further on the plans, and they did not shy away as the details unfolded. In fact, they became more intrigued with the premise. As they also grew older, they knew they could not keep up with the rigors of the culinary demands imposed by the cruise lines and the resorts. They also liked that they could take the cats with them.

For a place, his preference would be somewhere in New England, but if that did not materialize he was open to other areas. He had been working with a specialized real estate company for over fifteen years that had agents throughout New England when one of the agents at long last came up with what seemed to be on paper the perfect place. Computer images supported that conclusion. It was an old church in New Hampshire that had been completely refurbished in the early 70s and turned into a Bed and Breakfast business.

Grady was glad he maintained a valid driver's license. He rented a car and drove to see it and it was as perfect as he hoped it would be. It was on a desolate road some distance from the closest small town. The grounds were a bit rundown but could easily be restored to beauty. The inside was divided into two master suites, three bedroom suites, a large kitchen and a beautiful dining area with a picture window facing out to the woods. It even had a rather large and quaint cemetery to the rear that stretched out into the back woods. The last burial there was in 1937. The cemetery was in rather good condition and just seemed to need a bunch of tombstones righted and a good weeding. Grady envisioned not too much additional attention as its purpose would be best served if it appeared to be somewhat in disuse. The cemetery along with an additional thirty-nine acres was part of the deal. The back ten acres was an intriguing type of marshland that bordered a desolate river. Evidently, the marsh had expanded over time and encompassed remnants of wheat fields the early settlers had cultivated. It might be eerie to some, but he was captivated by the wheat and other tall grasses, and when the wind blew they seemed to take on a character of their own. His offer was accepted since it was not the kind of place that would appeal to many others. Grady was sure the Humples would want the kitchen updated.

Grady easily came up with a name for the place – *INN ENDLESS TIME*. Guests would come, but not all would go. The ones not leaving would be immortalized, partaking in endless time.

TWO

The retirement papers were submitted, and his supervisor and fellow employees were not surprised when Grady declined a party or any farewell luncheon. He had always been considered a loner, if not outright strange. That was the way he wanted it and the way it was best to be. Any personal closeness prompts excessive conversations and increases the chances of having to give explanations. A secret future was best served by an unrevealed past.

He bought a car, and when Cuba and Hilda had a four-day break they drove to the Inn so they could see the place and list what needed to be done with the kitchen. Since their own retirement was a major consideration, they loved the setting, the place, and the huge kitchen. One of the master suites was more than adequate for them and the cats. They need only now await the completion of the update and furnishing of a future they could only have dreamed about.

After the thrift shop emptied his apartment, Grady loaded the car with personal items and the things he estimated he would need to be there until the Inn was ready. As he drove away the shell of his life was left behind. It was all going to be different now. A sign that he had seen once came to mind:

I may be retired
But I'm just getting started.

Grady had researched for some time to locate just the right decorator to bring the Inn to its desired prominence. Eileen Dewert had led the decoration of some of the most acclaimed resorts as well as Bed and Breakfast establishments throughout New England from her Boston base. He had to set up the appointment for her to come to the Inn six weeks in advance, paying all of her expenses including putting her up at the nearest motel which was some thirty miles away. It was worth it. She fell in love with the place and could not contain an enthusiasm lacking recently for decorating a place as wonderful as this. Personally, she was quite attractive and in conversation she let it be known that she was divorced and had no children.

Eileen's initial concept, which Grady liked, was to do the place as an authentic country inn with early American furniture and antique furnishings that would be eye-catching and conversation pieces. She warned that it would be costly but the results would be worth it. Any price shock was somewhat softened by before he left when Cuba and Hilda signed over to him nearly all of their life savings. The theory was as he espoused to Eileen that for this special undertaking there was no such thing as halfway.

Eileen measured all of the rooms and indicated she would return in the morning with some preliminary sketches of some of the main themes she had in mind. She wanted to sleep on it to refine the ideas. If Grady had been more experienced, he might have picked up on some of the looks and the things she said that were geared towards a personal interest in him. As it was, he was left with the impression she was a likeable person and she was going to do a good job.

As he tried to sleep that night, he did think about her in greater detail. There was no denying he was attracted to her and it was a novel and almost compelling feeling. He had not been with a woman since college days. He could not recall her name, but she had long black hair, dark eyes, and puffy lips. She was two years older than he was and much more experienced. She led him along patiently and he might have wanted to be with her on a more permanent basis but she was a free spirit who avoided entanglements of all sorts. Perhaps, retirement was going to offer more challenges than just the Inn.

The next morning, the signs were too obvious even for him to ignore. The slacks and baggy jacket Eileen had worn the day before was replaced by a tight skirt and frilly blouse that had the two top buttons open revealing a tantalizing cleavage. She had brought coffee and danish and they sat on the stone wall surrounding the veranda.

Her voice had taken on a huskiness. "This has to be the quietest place on earth."

"That it is. It is a novelty to me but has not taken me long to like it. In fact, I am already addicted to it."

"It should be a good draw for the right kind of people."

"I'm counting on it."

"It's not everybody's cup of tea. Yet, what some folks crave is total solitude without any distractions."

"Sounds like something I can advertise."

"Yes, you should. It is also something I very much appreciate."

"That's good to know."

"This is also a particularly beautiful place that gets more spectacular the longer you are exposed to it."

"Supports my reason for buying it."

"Even the cemetery has a certain charm. I never thought I would feel that way about death or dying being so close."

He smiled. "Death has a charm of its own."

If that surprised or upset her, she did not show it. "How come you never married?"

That was not the same kind of question about what he was going to do when he retired. "The forces just did not tempt it."

"What forces are those?"

"Evil forces behind a man on a mission."

She thought that he was referring to an obstacle getting in his way of the Inn ambition. "My marriage did not last long. Unless there are common goals, people drift apart."

"I can see that."

"I decided to wait until I get back to Boston to do some preliminary sketches. First thing to do is to get the place painted. I was thinking a tan, maybe a deeper tan than the ordinary. It is neutral and the furniture and objects should stand out nicely. How does that sound?"

"I told you I know nothing about any of this. You do your thing and I am sure it will be fine. I have already made arrangements for modernizing the kitchen as Cuba and Hilda want. You will meet them along the way."

"Good. I am sure I can find some local painters. I'll set that up and be here to supervise. I'll bring the sketches with me." After a pause, she decided she would throw caution to the wind. Even if obvious, she was at that stage of her life when being coy was a waste of energy. "I'll have a couple of beds moved in. No sense spending your money on motels and my driving sixty miles back and forth." An afterthought would seal her fate. "Plus, I really like it here, and I'll consider all of my visits as working vacations."

THREE

On the drive back to Boston, Eileen had ample time to sort out the varied thoughts doing battle in her mind. The hopes and fears that emerged in recent years had to be confronted now that an unusual opportunity was in the offing. After thirty years of being a specialized decorator, she was burnt out. In recent years, the work had become boring, nearly oppressive. True creativity requires enthusiasm and inspiration, qualities that had become elusive. She had done so much for others, the satisfaction and enrichment gained by customers ever being unimportant. There was a growing sense that it was overdue that she attain something for herself. There had been so many resorts and Bed and Breakfasts that had been brought to amazing life over the years, the idea had been with her for a long time that there might be place like that of her own not only to work on but to be her supportive interest in retirement. Of all of the settings and projects, none had captured her dreams and expectations as Inn Endless Time. A burgeoning feeling settling in her heart and mind was that this Inn was to be her destiny. It was presumptuous to think that way but she was no longer young, no longer able to fully restrain emotions. Working on the sketches further fueled her intentions.

Where the interest in the Inn ended and the one in Grady began was clouded, although it probably made little difference. Eileen, perhaps deceptively, envisioned the future involving both. It had been many years since she had met a man she found so appealing. The combination of his ruggedness and evident lack of worldliness in the romance department told her he was different. At times his thoughts appeared disjointed and it was difficult to follow the logic. Yet, that made him more interesting, more of a challenge. Her brief marriage had been so disappointing that it had sent shock waves through her system for a long time. She looked on Grady as part and parcel of the opportunity before her and the exhilaration was thereby doubled. It was time, well overdue, for her to take a risk. These feelings were a lot to grapple with and even that represented more excitement than she had known for what seemed forever.

As was her habit, Eileen was a regular at some of the high end auctions in the Boston area. Over the years, many an idea had surfaced by objects and collections being offered. One held a few days after her return to Boston turned out to be a double bonanza. It not only gave her an idea for a certain space in the Inn, but it presented the way to fill a good portion of it. A large number of older leather-bound books, many of them classics, came up at the auction as a single lot. She had the winning bid which, surprisingly, was a mere fraction of the value of the collection. The auction house agreed to hold them for shipment when she was ready. That prompted a sketch of a cozy reading nook in the Inn with the books lined on shelves and two easy chairs with ottomans before a large window. At the same auction, she had the winning bid on a few interesting antiques. These would go to the storage area she had until there was enough for transport to the Inn.

Grady telephoned Eileen with the telephone number when the Inn's equipment was installed. There was much to talk about so the lengthy conversation was pleasurable. As an avid reader, he liked the idea of a book nook and gasped at what she had paid for all of the books. She had found a painter about an hour away who could bring along two helpers when the painting date was set.

Two weeks later, Eileen attended another auction and was able to successfully bid on two beds and some coverlets. A trucking company was hired to take the beds to the Inn. Then, the date for the painting to commence was arranged for.

In the meantime, Grady was doing work on the outside of the Inn. It certainly was a contrast for the many years he had lived in the city and worked in a confined office, but since he knew about plants it became an enjoyable task. Trimming, weeding, and mulching almost seemed like a natural activity. He most relished stomping out the walking trails which had become overgrown, and he would walk them frequently when the weather was favorable. Since the marsh had a particular fascination for him, he built a seating area on a ledge overlooking the expanse so that he could stare out and watch nature unfolding in various elements.

What surprised him the most was how often he thought about Eileen. From the extended period in his life when he occasionally would have appreciated a taste of romance, a constant desire was now engulfing his projections. At his age he would have thought there would be even less desires, and he wondered how many surprises were in store for him now that he had entered this new phase of his thinking and doing. When the beds arrived, that prompted even further selfish feelings. He stared at the Inn's sign that had just been installed, *INN ENDLESS TIME*, and it had an additional meaning than the subtle reference to the retirement goal.

The beds and coverlets arrived and were placed in the master suites. Grady made the forty-five mile trip to the nearest mall and bought pillows and sheets. He would await Eileen's arrival to make up the beds as he was not good at doing that. It would be good to give up sleeping on the air mattress he had brought with him.

Eileen showed up the day before the painters were scheduled to commence the work. She was dressed for the country, including jeans and a flannel shirt. She looked fresh and there was no denying the glow in her cheeks. They hugged, reluctant to break apart. She spoke first, "I missed this wonderful place. Of all the places I have seen and worked on, this one has made the most impression on me. It is not only beautiful but I feel a certain comfort here."

His smile was answer enough, but the words expressed his thoughts. "That's awfully nice to hear."

"I have also looked forward to being with you."

"Likewise." He held her body closer, fully aware of her body contours. "I can certainly use your help."

That was not the kind of committal she wanted, but she sensed he was naturally guarded. "This is a working vacation, so I'll enjoy all that comes with it." Subtlety was not the avenue to her expectations. "I stopped for some sandwiches."

They ate on the veranda, the warm sunlight framing the casual conversation. He brought her things into the bedroom he was using, not thinking twice about it.

Before viewing the sketches, they walked the trails. Eileen was enraptured by the beauty and the serenity. The silence was captivating, and even an occasional bird's song merely accentuated the quietness. If the trails would be any indication, the Inn would certainly capture endless time.

Just as they rounded a bend in the path, she stumbled on a rock. He caught her before she fell, and they eased into a warm embrace capped by a tender kiss. A more ardent kiss followed. One would think they were teenagers. Newness is provocative at any age.

The sketches brought further excitement to the venture. He remarked how talented and creative she was, and she was sure she was blushing.

Without any prudish preliminaries, they slept in the same bed. In its own right, the act of love was satisfying. Upon awakening in the morning, she had not planned on asking it but the idea came out anyway. "After I assemble all I need and accomplish what has to be done in Boston, I would like to be here with you."

This was a far distance from his long established plans, and it flashed through his mind that it might well represent a major impediment. Yet, he could not deny he wanted her probably as much as effectuating the scheme. "I would like that. I would like it very much." He envisioned it as a problem then only if she did not fall in with the overall plan. If she balked at it, he would have to handle it then.

FOUR

Four days later the painting was completed. The wide plank flooring probably could have used some refinishing, but Eileen was planning to cover a major portion of them with colorful early braided rugs. The kitchen suppliers had shown up and installed all of the ordered equipment. Cuba and Hilda would be pleased.

"It's starting to come together." Grady reached for her hand and fingers entwined. "I guess I never saw a dream come true before."

Eileen smiled. "You ain't seen anything yet. Just wait until the things I have been ordering with my laptop start filling up this place. You may faint when you see the bills, but this will transform this place into a magical inn. The past will be created with stepping stones to the future."

"Do you think we can open by spring?"

"Sure."

"We'll have to work on an advertisement to place in the exclusive travel magazines, as well as a personal letter to the list of contacts I have compiled over the years. At some point, I need to go to Washington to talk personally with certain people."

"Sounds ominous."

"Could be."

"Maybe you should rename the inn as *Inn of Mystery.*"

"If inns could have a subtitle that might be quite appropriate."

"I don't frighten easily."

"That's good to know."

"Others might be."

"I'm counting on that."

"I think more than the inn, you are a man of mystery."

"Might be."

"I just hope it all has a happy ending."

"For you, yes. For others, maybe not so much."

She glanced around almost as if someone might be eavesdropping. In a whisper, she responded tentatively, "Are there things you are not telling me?"

"Just by being here, you will know it all."

"What if I am impatient?"

"Then you will see it all but understand little."

"I hope, at least, I can understand you a little."

"It might take some doing."

"I'm up to it."

He was silent for a moment. It might be too soon to tell her what was going to be involved, but since it would probably be a shock to her it might be best if he started to clear the way. "What are you expecting to find here, Eileen?"

She did not answer immediately, but she wanted to be honest with him and herself. "I am not really expecting anything. I hope to find my future. I have dreamed of having a place like this for my retired years. After meeting you, I am hoping there is a compatibility for us to share in this place, its promise, and in each other. I have money to help along the way."

"And what if I tell you there is more involved in all of this than meets the eye? What if I tell you there is much more to know about this place and me before you commit to be a part of it?"

"Here comes the man of mystery again."

"I just don't want you to imagine what may not be here. For instance, I am a very simple person, probably boring after awhile to someone as sophisticated as you."

"Do I come across as a snob?"

"No, but a man with broader interests might be more entertaining."

"At my age, entertainment is not on my needs list. I suspect you are making things sound more complicated than they need be."

He decided he had said enough to this point. After all, she might well tire of this place or with him before the Inn opened and go on to other ventures. Then there would be no need for particulars. He also did not know her well enough yet to get a feel for whether he could trust her with the pervasive details and whether she could handle them.

Plans and expectations had gestated for too many years for a divergence. He decided to take it all just one step at a time. He would enjoy her company and appreciate her efforts at making the inn an enticing place.

A walk through the paths eased the moment. Holding hands, they sat by the marsh enthralled by the vista. Then they lingered in the cemetery reading the headstones. Those buried there would be silent witnesses to whatever transpired here.

FIVE

Working as a team, they set furniture and objects in place as the deliveries came in. Most enjoyable was the book arranging when the boxes of leather books arrived. Grady spent as much time reading as he did placing them on the shelves of the antique bookcases Eileen had found.

The brochure also took on a life of its own.

Do you need or want to escape the entrapments of this mad world?

Do you want to experience a totally private and peaceful environment?

Inn Endless Time is an adult paradise.
It is a forgotten place where time and existence are put on hold.

Select a book from and read it in the comfortable book nook.

Indulge in gourmet meals prepared by our award winning resident chefs.
Dine alone or with others.

Walk extensive nature trails away from prying eyes, ears, and minds.

All degrees of solitude are possible, and you can try them all.

No routines; no schedules; no rules.
No one will bother you. Be yourself as you may have always wanted to be.

Come for a weekend, for a week, for a month, or for a lifetime.

Entering the Inn and your prior world will be left behind. No computers, phones, or other devices are allowed. There are no televisions, radios, or clocks in the rooms.
There is no way to calculate or capture endless time.
Reservations are required. No credit cards or checks accepted. Cash only.
800-972-1868

Cuba and Hilda moved all of their possessions in and began serving their last winter on a cruise ship as Grady took care of the cats, and they were glad they no longer had to board the felines since Grady was at the Inn. They had felt bad for the cats and it was expensive for such long periods. They met and liked Eileen and were confident Grady would win her over when he announced she had not yet been briefed on the true aim of the Inn.

Grady had decided to run the Inn on a regular basis for a year before commencing the special visits. That way routine and reputation should be firmly established so that once the extra activity commenced it might not be noticed. This would also give him more time to ease Eileen to acceptance of the true purpose of the plan. Perhaps by then she would be so accustomed to the operation of the Inn that any additional program would be as an afterthought. Endless time can have many facets.

At the grand opening in the spring the place looked spectacular and was booked two months in advance. Full booking was not overly burdensome with only three rooms available.

Cuba and Hilda's preparation and presentation of sensational meals nearly guaranteed continued high guest potential. Eileen had created a special cozy dining area that was fashioned after an early tavern setting, replicating what would have been a stage coach stop. The ambiance added just the right touch to the bountiful feasts. A side benefit was that Grady and Eileen had some wonderful food to indulge in. Besides other chores, walking the paths regularly became necessary to keep weight gain at a minimum.

In the second month a real positive boost came with a rebooking. If a guest wanted to come back that soon, something was being done right. Actually, it turned out to represent what might be an interesting variation on Grady's long-range scheme. The guest was Tessie Alveni, and only after engaging her in conversation during her second stay of a week did he find out that she was the wife of Salvatore Domano, a reputed crime boss in New York City. He had been looking for a safe place to send her periodically. She drove herself and was quite adept at avoiding being followed. This was made easier on the seemingly endless series of country roads leading to the Inn. The criminal element would probably fall all over themselves for the kind of services Grady was going to offer, but that would likely never happen. His primary design was for a higher purpose. Yet, he would welcome Tessie whenever she wanted to be at the Inn, and he knew she liked the pampered atmosphere. It was a win-win situation.

Eileen would have guessed that Mrs. Alveni would have preferred a full service hotel with more activities and a greater social situation. Yet, probably the last thing a woman can figure out is what another woman prefers, or is led to prefer.

SIX

A travel magazine sent a representative to spend a couple of days at the Inn. The ensuing published article was highly favorable. After raving about the food, it touted the place as an oasis in an otherwise dry environment of so-called escape destinations.

The loving relationship between Grady and Eileen was becoming closer and more significant. For Grady, the absence of an emotional involvement for so many years brought forth feelings that he thought he was not capable of. He had rationalized for such a long time that he did not need a romantic tie that it was a form of shock to his entire being that he not only liked such a feeling but actually wanted it. For Eileen, the past disappointments in her life of the men she had been involved with were dissipated by this new man. He was caring and attentive, and to her delight she kept discovering characteristics which were entertaining and illustrative of sensitive capabilities that would melt the heart of a woman craving that in a man.

Grady held several private strategy sessions with Cuba and Hilda on how disappearances and disposal might be handled. Unison with a defined purpose would be necessary, and there was complete agreement to do whatever implementation was required and with whatever specifics might develop along the way. The first instance would be a test case and refinements would follow.

The Inn was booked all summer, and then the autumn colors prompted bookings and even a waiting list. Success was an elixir carrying them through the absorption of time and expenditure of energy. Grady had initially estimated that the ordinary operation of the Inn would be just a coverup and that it was the special activity that would be the money maker. As it turned out, the Inn was already highly successful. One truism kept repeating itself – the wealthy are willing to pay for whatever they think they want and need.

Grady knew it was inevitable that Eileen be told the truth. He loved her and would hate to lose her, but there would be no way to hide it from her. If he explained it the right way and could persuade her of his firm beliefs then her love for him might lead to acceptance. He decided it would be more difficult to do if he waited any longer.

It was a beautiful fall day. The chill in the air was chased away by the lingering fragments of the summer sun. There were no guests at the Inn that day so he suggested to her that they take a walk.

Hand-in-hand they walked one of the pathways for a bit. When they came across a large rock on the side he suggested they sit on it. He was still holding her hand and it felt warm and firm. "There is something important you need to know. Actually, there are two things. The first is that for a very long time I did not believe I needed to have someone to love and to love me. I was guided and totally absorbed in the dream of an inn that I did not think I needed anything or anyone else. Now that I have shared this dream with you, I realize that it means so much more that way. Without qualification I can say I truly love you."

Eileen smiled and squeezed his hand. "And I love you very much."

"The other thing is going to take some explaining so please hear me out before you say anything. In fact, you may want to think about it before you say anything. It will take some thinking to digest all of its implications." He took a deep breath hoping the words and ideas would come out the right way and that she would be receptive to them. "While the dream of the Inn changed over the years, the idea was actually founded on another plan. I stumbled upon a motive soon after I started working on Capitol Hill. I happened to overhear a secret conversation about a special need this country has. Such a concept was reinforced in thoughts, expressed and implied, over the years. There are persons who represent a threat to this nation and to the American way of life. A way of removing them would go a long way in diminishing such threats. A way of making them disappear would be perfect. A desolate Inn is a way to accomplish that."

Eileen gasped as she let go of his hand. Her exclamation was probably what he should have expected yet he was not fully prepared for it. "You can't be serious!"

He thought it best to continue as if she had not interrupted him. "Over the Winter I will visit and approach the people and organizations who will be receptive to this idea. I have had many years to compile such a list. There are more than you might think. They will pay handsomely for such a service while we will be performing a patriotic duty. It must sound drastic to you but it is well thought out and what has to be considered a necessary evil."

"Drastic is an understatement! I am shocked. It is all deeply troubling to me. The biggest point is that I see in you a quality I had not seen before and do not approve of. Is there anything I can say that would dissuade you from such a cockeyed scheme?"

"I doubt it. As with any new idea, perhaps you need to take some time to think about it."

"It is an idea totally foreign to my view of life. Are Cuba and Hilda aware of this?"

"Yes, they are completely on board with it. This place is their ideal retirement. They get to cook what they want without any financial restrictions and without the stress of cruise line schedules and rules, and not having to deal with all sorts of kitchen personnel. They have their own private and comfortable quarters and a cozy place for the cats. They have no problem with the concept and will do whatever I ask of them."

"Listen carefully to me, Grady. The whole idea makes no sense. It is not reasonable, especially in the light of what you will be jeopardizing. This place is already a success and a money maker. We can enjoy a comfortable old age together with the added stimulation of what these surroundings give us. If you get involved in something illegal and get caught you will be giving all of this up. Even if you get away with it you will have no peace and will be looking over your shoulder constantly."

"Wealth is just part of the story. Something positive for the well being of our country is involved. Besides, if it is not done here someone else will eventually do it and reap the rewards and satisfaction."

"Being stubborn can make you blind to the many negatives. Realistically, how do you expect to get away with it?"

"There are many ways to arrange for accidents. There are also many undetectable poisons that can be put in food and drinks."

"What will you do with the bodies?"

"The cemetery is a bonanza. The marsh can also hide things where others will not venture."

"Someone will know that the person was here. Suspicion will grow as the numbers grow. There will be constant questioning and investigations, and eventually the pieces will be put together. You can't just keep making people disappear. Do you really want to spend the rest of your life in prison rather than here?"

"It will all be well planned. The powers that request such a fate will protect us."

"Grady, you can't be that naive. You'll be tossed to the wolves whenever anything goes wrong. And, things will go wrong. Do you really want to turn this magnificent place into a murder camp?"

Grady was silent. He figured it would take some convincing for Eileen to accept an idea now evidently so radical to her way of thinking. He underestimated the strength of her opposition. Maybe he should not push it anymore for the moment. "I'll think about what you said."

Her voice softened considerably. "Above everything else, I am against anything that puts our love in jeopardy."

"I value that. We'll talk some more."

"Promise me we will talk much more before you do anything."

He embraced her. "I promise."

SEVEN

Over the next few days Grady did give much thought to all Eileen had said. He could not deny it made a great deal of sense, especially since he was deriving so much satisfaction from the normal operation of the Inn. Yet, that might be due in large part to the still novel activity of being such an entrepreneur, and he was not sure he was ready to completely abandon what he had spent a life time preparing for. Looking back on all the sacrifices he had made to realize a plan he had been convinced was best for him and for the country, would it be possible to wipe the slate clean and adjust to a realization that it might all have been in vain? He was also well aware that it was not the Inn that had altered his outlook. It was the love that he felt for this woman who had awakened the vibrant sensations of his new being. Perhaps, it had been a crucial mistake to have denied himself of a love interest over all of those years so that this newness would not have had such a strong impact.

Eileen had said nothing further, and she behaved as if the conversation had never taken place. She was loving and attentive as usual, and would reach for his hand whenever possible. One of the great strengths that she had relied on all of her life had been the philosophy that if something was meant to be then it would work out that way. In a way, this love was new to her as well, and she basked in the splendor of the vibrant moments.

In bed, he held her close, caressing the soft skin. "Thank you for being patient with me."

She put her warm hand on his chest. "I know you will tell

me when you are ready."

"I need to be as honest with you as I must be to myself. Each day I realize the love I feel for you brings me great contentment. I will give up on this plan for now, but I can't say forever."

Eileen was thrilled because it was more of a concession than she had dared to hope for. "I accept that, and I love you that much more because I know you are doing it for me." She was convinced that time and events would solidify his decision. "You may also realize at some point that you are doing it for yourself as well."

"I am doing it for us. Us and the Inn have become one in my heart."

"I can't tell you how pleased I am to hear this. I feel the same way. We must be doing something right."

Grady thought he better not say anymore. If one repeats things too much they have a tendency to sound insincere. He was not as sure of the future as the present, but that was better left unsaid.

In the morning, as had become an enjoyable routine, they had coffee in the book nook while nibbling on one of Hilda's pastry creations. No wonder guests raved about them as she came up with an unusual variety of tastes and designs.

They embraced warmly before going to make up a suite that a guest had just vacated. They worked well as a team, and that was reassuring in its own right. Then they took a long walk hand-in-hand to ward off any extra weight the pastry might add.

Tessie Alveni came for her third stay, and she could hardly contain her excitement about being there. It was a place she lounged in quality rest while feeling safer than anywhere else. There were always too many lurking shadows in the city and other places she might frequent, and Sal was after her constantly to be on guard, so much so that she barely could enjoy any place or activity. Contrary forces knew she was a weak spot in his life and operations, and attacking her could be a way of getting at him. Tessie was also wild about the food. Cuba's culinary creations were what she eagerly looked forward to, and Hilda's popovers were on her favorites list. She tried to keep the weight off, but at age fifty she felt she was entitled to a little plumpness. Out of caution, she had given up so many other things but these feasts were irresistible.

After breakfast on her second day at the Inn, Tessie approached Grady as he was sweeping the entrance way. She invited him to take a walk with her. He agreed and first went to tell Eileen who was cleaning the book nook. Raised eyebrows was her silent reaction.

They walked for awhile in silence. The autumn air was crisp although the sun still maintained an inherent warmth. Newly fallen leaves crunched beneath their footsteps. He glanced sideways at her and realized he could not even begin to guess how old she was. She was not a beauty, although she could turn heads. There were some fine lines in her face but the skin was taut. She was a bit plump although it seemed to be more alluring than a turn off. Her clothing was this day as well as all of the other times she frequented the Inn a perfect fit, appealing, and undoubtedly expensive. They may very well have been made especially for her. Grady guessed that even the sneakers she was wearing along with the wool suit were the best that money could buy.

She noticed his glance at her. "Don't try to figure me out. There is much more about me than you can see."

"I have no doubt about that. I have already determined you are smarter than I am."

"Smart does not always prevail."

He grimaced. "Tell me something I don't already know."

"There are different kinds of smart as well."

"For sure."

"Sal has an uncanny ability to figure out how events will unfold. He is also right ninety-nine percent of the time about a person's character. He knows right off the bat who he can trust."

"Comes in handy for him, no doubt."

"No doubt. I don't have that same ability, but I do know who I like. And, I like you and Eileen. Have you known each other for a long time?"

"No. The Inn has brought us together. A mutual enterprise can do that. Have you been married for a long time?"

"We grew up in the same neighborhood. We are not married."

"Oh."

"Everyone thinks we are. That's where he is not smart. He thinks that if I am not his wife it makes me safe from his enemies. As long as we are together, and it has been many, many years, I am as vulnerable as if I were his wife."

"I can understand that. Of course, you must know that without being married you are without certain rights."

"He has made provisions over the years for me to have money of my own."

"As long as you are satisfied with the arrangement, it's not for me to say anything." He had an idea that this conversation would make him think about his relationship with Eileen.

As if she was reading his mind, she inquired, "Are you and Eileen married?"

"No. We are married to the Inn."

"Do you want to know why I asked you to take a walk with me?"

"It's not anything I can guess at."

"Since I like you, I feel I can trust you. Can I?"

"Probably."

"Probably?"

"I cannot commit to a blanket trust until I know what we are talking about."

"I pegged you right. You are smart, too."

"Maybe too smart for my own good."

"No sense mincing words. I like it here. I really, really like it here. Sal and I have devised this plan. We would fake my suicide and I would get some plastic surgery to alter my appearance and disappear. I would like to disappear here. I know I would be forever happy here. It is beautiful and quiet. I feel comfortable with the surroundings and you all. I won't be any trouble, and I will help out, even as a chambermaid. I don't shy away from work, even difficult work. There will be a bundle of money in it for you. Outside of here, only Sal would know. Sal and I are resigned not to ever be together again, and his peace of mind will work for him as well as for me. I assume if I can trust you I can also trust Eileen and your kitchen magicians."

Grady was quiet for a moment. "Wow! This is a lot to digest. Naturally, I would have to talk it over with Eileen as well as with Cuba and Hilda. All would have to agree to it. This is a mutual operation and there can be no secrets among ourselves."

Tessie put her hand on his arm. "Be convincing. This is the perfect answer for me and I will do whatever it takes to make it work out."

"I'll let you know by tomorrow, hopefully."

"Good."

They continued walking in silence. Grady's mind was racing, and after a major part of a lifetime with little excitement or surprises he could hardly believe that life could be so unpredictable.

Eileen edged close to him when he returned to the Inn. "Well, what was all that about?"

"You'll find out tonight when we have a kitchen meeting with Cuba and Hilda."

"I don't get a preview?"

"A little suspense will get you more interested in me."

"There is no more room at the Inn. My interest in you is already at its peak."

EIGHT

After Cuba and Hilda had cleaned up the kitchen from dinner, Grady assembled the Inn Endless Time ensemble in the kitchen. They sat in chairs around the cleared end of the long work table which was otherwise stacked with dishes as well as the pots and pans and cooking utensils that were not hung up around the kitchen walls. The overhead lights were very bright so Grady was sure he would be able to note facial expressions. "I suppose we should meet more often like this as it caps my feelings that our operation runs like a well-oiled machine. I appreciate and love each one of you. But, there is a special reason that has arisen for our gathering. When a decision has to be made about the Inn and our lives here, it demands a discussion and agreement by all. At her request, I walked with Tessie Alveni today, and she has made an unusual proposal. I don't know how to explain it except as she stated it to me." He then carefully repeated all that she had said.

The end of his narration was greeted by complete silence. It had been quite a bit to digest, and he was not sure he had processed all of the nuances.

Cuba spoke up, his deep resonating voice commanding a degree of authority. Grady imagined how the kitchen staff on the cruises and at the hotels must have jumped into action upon his commands. "I believe I speak for Hilda as well. If not, as you well know, she will not stay quiet. You are our main man. Whatever you decide about this is fine." He glanced at Hilda who nodded before he continued. "We are happy here. We have our space, our cats, and complete freedom in the kitchen to do what we love. We cook what we want and at our own pace, a far cry from the harsh demands of our former life. You have made this possible. So, whatever you want to do with this lady or otherwise, you can count on us."

Hilda chimed in, "I couldn't have said it better. We also appreciate you confiding in us and wanting our opinion. We are committed for the long haul. We will do whatever and whenever you need."

Grady was touched by the outpouring of support, and it once again confirmed that his choice of these two was the very best he could have done. These long time friends were wonderful people, and having them near was doing more for him than he was doing for them.

They all looked at Eileen. She glanced from one to the other before she spoke. "I thought your original scheme was, to say the least, unusual. This is also way out there, although it is something I can probably live with if it is completely feasible. I have no idea whether aiding and abetting one to disappear is a crime. I am not sure it is workable for us. We only have three guest suites. If one gets occupied permanently, we are down to two. It detracts from our inn scope. Even with three it is difficult to keep up with the demand so far. Having an influx of different people at different times adds to the interest and design of what we do and what we stand for. That is just one aspect. What happens if it does not work out for us? Can we end the arrangement, or does she expect it to be final? Exactly what kind of money is she talking about considering how much of the inn operation will be affected? And, I suppose the most crucial aspect is how successful her so-called disappearance will be? Just to conceive of such a plan indicates to me that there is some great danger in her life and that those who might want to find her are dangerous. There may be a good deal of risk at some point for us, and it would be a concern that will be there every day."

Grady cleared his throat. "My dear, you sure are the voice of reason, and you bring up good points. I suggest I go get her and bring her here to answer such concerns. I suppose there is also a need to know the timing of all of this."

"I'll get her," Eileen offered.

While she was gone, Hilda spoke on another topic. "We really like Eileen. Grady, she is a keeper. She fits right in."

"Yes," Grady responded, "I lucked out with her just as I did with the two of you."

Eileen returned with Tessie in tow. A fifth chair had been put at the table and Grady motioned for Tessie to occupy it. "We have some concerns that you can speak to."

"I expected that you would. So would I if I were in your shoes. I'll try to respond as best that I can, but some details at my end have not yet been fully determined. Also, I realize that if you go along with this that there will probably be some other things that develop along the way that will have to be agreed to. I promise I will be as flexible and cooperative as possible. After all, you are going way out of your way on my account."

"That's encouraging," Grady said. "Of course, the major concern is the safety of all of us and the Inn. How sure are you that you will not be found here?"

"There can be no absolute certainties. I know that. Sal is the only other person who will know, and I assure you he will never reveal anything. I have already been extra careful about coming here. After the surgery, and there has been no time set for it yet, no one will be able to recognize me. Even you will think I am a new person, and in a way I will be."

"Then there is the matter of giving up one of the suites for you. That is a great limitation for other guests since we only have three."

Tessie was silent for a moment. "I have given some thought to that already. I have the idea of completely financing an addition to the Inn, including the furnishings. Would that work for you?"

"What do you mean exactly?", Eileen blurted out.

"You can determine the size, location, and compatible style. You will wind up with extra rooms for guests. More income to boot."

"It might be real expensive," Grady interjected. "We might need a new well and a septic system for sure."

"Not a problem."

"And the cost of you being here?"

"We can set a fair amount less any money I may work for."

"What happens if it does not work out for either or both of us?"

"I walk away and the addition is all yours."

"Where does the money come from?"

"There are a series of untraceable offshore bank accounts solely in my name. Any money for the Inn would be deposited directly into the Inn's account.'"

Grady looked to the others. "Any other questions?" All shook their heads. "Well, Tessie, Eileen will see you back to your suite and we'll ponder this some more."

Tessie rose from the chair. "I can find my own way. I appreciate you considering this. It is much to chew on, I know. Good night."

After she left, Grady turned to Cuba. "How many more guests can you accommodate in the kitchen?"

Cuba rubbed his large chin. "We are used to preparing for crowds, but you want to keep it within the limits of the equipment. I would say eight more at the most, which means four rooms more if at double occupancy. The real problem is the dining room. If we are full you will have to have staggered seatings. It also puts a strain on the serving which you and Eileen are doing now."

Grady turned to Eileen. "What are your thoughts?"

"Not that I am greedy, but the money is tempting particularly if we get an addition with furnishings and we get really successful. Knowing we have a steady source of income is enticing. I am not sold completely on the idea, and just hope it is not too good to be true. The big question that pops up, is she telling us everything? If we do take a chance on this we have to consider safeguards. We are out in the boonies."

"All good points. Let's sleep on it and meet again after breakfast."

In bed, Eileen turned to Grady and knew he was awake and probably having trouble sleeping just as she was. "Do we take this leap of faith or just go with whatever comes our way?"

He kissed her forehead. "Not an easy question to answer. Seems to me a chance either way. We can crash on our own or grab the gold ring and then crash?"

"Then what happens to the gold ring?"

NINE

The group met after breakfast. With no new thoughts surfacing it was decided to go ahead with Tessie's disappearance scheme as long as they could get the maximum details and assurances.

It was a cloudy and breezy day. Grady suggested to Tessie that they take a walk to the marsh to watch the tall grasses blow in different directions by the wind, almost as if they took on a life of their own. They sat on the ledge in the area Grady had created. "Well, Tessie, as soon as you have all of the details in place let us know. Unless something comes up that we haven't discussed, we are inclined to go along with your plan. You have told us everything, haven't you?"

Tessie smiled and reached for his hand, "For letting me disappear into your lives, I won't hold anything back. As soon as you get an estimate for the addition and its contents, I'll deposit that amount in the account. That will be my offering of good intentions. As you know, there are no guarantees in life. Sal and I have planned this well. The only piece missing was you. It will work out for all of us. That is what we have to believe to maximize the results." Before she let go of his hand he noticed a jagged scar on her wrist where the sleeve of her sweater had lifted up on the outstretched arm. He imagined it came from growing up in a tough neighborhood. She had probably been fighting most of her life for a smattering of dignity. For a moment he imagined there were others who wanted or needed to disappear if they had the resources to effectuate it. Maybe that was going to be the true destiny of the Inn of Endless Time. His mind had been going through a series of adjustments recently, and he had the feeling that this was not the end of the story.

Eileen emailed a picture of the Inn to an architect in Boston that she had worked with before, and the woman came up with a compatible addition attached to one end of the existing Inn with four suites. It was determined that the existing well was adequate but a separate septic system would be needed for the addition. Eileen started searching the online auctions for the antique furnishings.

When everything was tallied up, with construction to begin in the spring, it came to $70,000. Grady was sure Tessie would balk at this staggering amount, but when he talked to her on the secure telephone line she had given him and he explained the cost was so much higher because the construction crew and materials had to travel some distance to get there, she did not hesitate or question it. She said she would start immediately to have staggered small amounts transferred to the Inn's account until the total was reached. This would raise the least suspicion. She stated her preference for having one of the suites in the main house since guest suites would then be available in what they were already calling the Annex. Grady did not have a problem with that. The conversation ended with Tessie promising to give him advance notice whenever the event was scheduled.

The winter was cold and snowy. The county did a good job plowing the roads and keeping them passable most of the time. Deliveries to the Inn were not affected. To their delight, the Inn had at least one guest at any given time throughout the long winter months. The slower pace was enjoyable and relaxing. Grady and Eileen had many meaningful moments to themselves, and it was especially significant that they did not tire of each other. Cuba and Hilda had many extended periods with the cats, and when in the kitchen they had ample opportunities to experiment with culinary masterpieces. That was a favorite pastime. Grady and Eileen were the true beneficiaries of such activity.

True to her word, Tessie effectuated sufficient funds

deposited for the construction endeavor. The first task as spring arrived and the ground thawed was installation of the septic system for the Annex. Then just as the framing for the addition went up, Tessie announced her permanent arrival the next week.

They were all prepared for a drastic change in her appearance, but it was still a shock to see her standing before them. It was as if a stranger had showed up on the doorstep. Even the plumpness was gone. The facial features were completely different, eye-color was changed, and an altered color of the hair. Her voice and mannerism were also different. For all intents and purposes this was a new person. Besides an abundance of clothing, it appeared as if she had not brought many personal items. She announced her new name as Victoria Caulfield, and she requested to be called Vicky.

Eileen said it best. "Tessie has truly disappeared. I can't believe Vicky is the same person."

Grady added, "We better get used to it. This is how it is."

Grady and Eileen had already discussed how Vicky could do work at the Inn. Serving in the dining room when occupancy required staggered meal sittings as well as making up rooms would be the primary functions. Since she had also offered to do work outside, there were always things that required upkeep so when there was no need for other duties she would do that.

They had thought about getting a watch dog, but it was decided that such might infringe on the quietness and raise concern by some guests. Instead, they had a sophisticated unobtrusive security system installed. Of course, it was not fool proof although it furnished some degree of reassurance.

Vicky was no trouble at all. She did all that was asked of her. She ate most of her meals in her room, and did not mingle with any of the guests. Her appetite did not seem to be as robust as in earlier times, but they figured she was trying to be disciplined and to keep the weight off. She even limited her intake of Hilda's popovers.

By mid-summer all of the construction had been completed and Eileen's vigil in obtaining the most unusual of furnishings was fully accomplished. Increased capacity meant they could accommodate more guests, and there was no problem in filling up the place. A waiting list was a constant feature. Success was beyond their fondest dreams.

Along with increased success, the love shared by Grady and Eileen grew along with it. One day as they sat by the marsh, Eileen squeezed his hand and put it to her lips. "I not only love you but you make me so happy. It is too bad we did not meet earlier in life so we could have had more time together."

"I doubt you would have been attracted to a lowly parliamentarian."

"The magic would have been there."

Grady had been thinking about asking her to marry him, and this seemed to be as good a time as any. "I want to ask you something."

"Let me ask you something first."

"O.K."

"I want our love to last for endless time as is our Inn. It is our Inn, right?"

"Of course. What is mine is yours."

"Good. I wanted to have that point settled. Will you marry me?"

He laughed loudly. "It is not polite to take the words out of my mouth. That is just what I was going to ask you."

She giggled. "Just proves that great minds run in tandem."

"History will show this as the first double proposal at a marshland."

"Not quite. I believe that was the invention of the marshmallow."

He appreciated her sense of humor along with everything else. She was good for him. He had been far too serious all of his life. There is so much truth to the concept that crying and laughing are good for people. "Maybe I should call you Marsha from now on."

A month later they married with a simple civil ceremony in the book nook performed by a Justice of the Peace. Cuba, Hilda, and Vicky looked on. A kiss sealed the marriage pact. Cuba and Hilda prepared a special wedding feast, capped by a cake Hilda had never made before and which was as delicious as it was beautiful to look at. On the top was a replica of the Inn, and written below in icing was Love and Happiness Inn Endless Time.

TEN

Most lovers will agree that true love does not guarantee a problem free life. Or, maybe another truism kicks in. When things are going too good prepare for the worst.

It was a particularly beautiful late summer day. The Inn was full, and the guests were interesting and enjoying the serenity that the Inn touted. Grady was trimming the bushes on the side of the Inn. Vicky was helping him by gathering the cut parts and placing them in a wheel barrow which Grady would take into the woods to dump when it was full. She was wearing jeans and a tee shirt. He happened to glance down just as she was reaching for a pile next to him when it struck him that there was no scar on her wrist. All sorts of thoughts raced through his mind. Since she had plastic surgery perhaps she had the scar removed at the same time. After all, it may have bothered her or been a constant reminder of a tortuous youth. Or, had they been too trusting? Was Vicky not Tessie after all?

He tried to keep his composure until the trimming was completed. After he dumped the cuttings deep in the woods he rushed in to tell Eileen. She was straightening out the dining area. He led her to their room, and after closing the door he expressed his concerns.

"Now that you have discovered this," Eileen whispered, "I have been wrestling with the fact that there are just too many different personality quirks that Vicky has. I have been uncomfortable with it."

"What or why I keep asking myself."

"I fully understand. Think hard, as we should not do anything about this until we are absolutely sure about it. Is there anything that only Tessie would know about the Inn or us from her early visits that Vicky would be unaware of?"

Grady was silent as he prodded his memory. "I can't think of a thing. Tessie once asked me how we met, but we were interrupted and I never did get to tell her."

"Then we have to be creative and present it as if it had happened and see how she reacts."

"Do you think she might be dangerous if cornered?"

Eileen reached for his hand. "There is always that possibility, I suppose. But, if we are right, lots of trouble is behind this as well as a great deal of money and I can't see her jeopardizing it."

"I don't think we should say anything to Cuba and Hilda just yet."

"I agree."

"Of course, finding out if she is Tessie or not is only half of the problem. The other is what we do about it."

"We'll face that when and if we have to. Some problems do resolve themselves."

"I hope."

After further discussion, they devised a plan that they thought might bring the matter to a head. They would ask Vicky to accompany them to the site where Grady had made a sitting ledge at the marsh to get her opinion about making it a more intriguing place for guests to walk to.

After all of the lunch serving and cleaning up duties were done, they asked Vicky to go with them to the marsh. She agreed and they set out after freshening up. They made some small talk along the way. A snake slithered across their path at one point eager to get to the woods as if it knew something sinister was about to happen.

At the marsh, they sat upon the ledge Grady had set up with the wide expanse of the marsh before them. When they were completely settled, taking in the mysterious vista for a few minutes, Grady spoke firmly. "In a nutshell here is my idea. We erect a railing for guests to lean against as they strain to see in as far as possible. A board will be attached to the tree to the left here which will detail the legend of the marsh as the former owners conveyed to me. Vicky, you were very intrigued by it when I told you about it last fall, and I am sure other guests will get swept up in it as well. At the same time as the famous Salem witch hunts, the frenzy spread even as far as here. Locals believed a coven was nearby. Several young girls suspected of being witches were burned at the stake. Their remains were buried in the cemetery behind the Inn and which accounts for the graves with blank tombstones. A few other tormented girls fled to the marsh and were never found. Belief is that they died here and that when the wind blows their spirits cause the grasses to blow in various directions."

As if on cue a breeze came up and the grasses instead of blowing in the direction of the wind blew in all different directions. They stared at the scene before them until the breeze died down.

"I think it is a great idea," Eileen offered.

Grady turned to Vicky. "Probably others will be taken with it as you are."

"I am sure," Vicky's voice was tentative or at least it seemed that way to Grady. "It will be a conversation piece alright. People can get swept up in things even if it is not the truth."

Grady was sure there was a hidden meaning behind her words, and the opening was too tempting for him to ignore. "And what is true, dear lady?"

Vicky sounded surprised by the question. "What do you mean?"

"I mean, I made all of this up. Tessie and I were here but there was no legend. We know you are not Tessie. Who are you?"

Vicky laughed. "If I have fooled you, nobody else will ever believe I am, or rather I was, Tessie."

"Eileen raised her voice close to a shouting pitch. "Enough of the charade. Please tell us what is going on here. There is much at risk."

Vicky was quiet, and she cast her eyes downward. "Alright.

I knew there would come a point I would have to tell you. It is just that things were going along so well I did not want to chance a blowup." She looked at Eileen and then at Grady. "I am Jean Alveni, Tessie's sister." She stopped as if that was all she needed to say.

"Please tell us everything," Grady pressed. "We have a right to know."

"Yes, I know you do." Vicky stared out over the marsh probably wanting to escape into it as the fictional persecuted girls did. "Even the best of plans have to be changed in the face of immediate life and death situations. All that Tessie had planned and told you was true, and she had every intention of carrying through with it. Then, I got into trouble, really bad trouble, and it is probably best you don't know the details, and there are some very bad people looking for me and who want me dead. There was no time for plastic surgery, and this is the real me. Tessie thought I would be safe here so she made me take her place. I do feel safe here, and I so much appreciate you taking me in even if you have been deceived to an extent. Instead of Tessie disappearing, I need to."

Grady was still uncertain this was the truth. "Are you wanted by the authorities? Harboring a criminal is illegal and we can get into a good deal of trouble."

"No, it is entirely a personal matter, and believe me it is far worse than being hunted by the police."

He continued. "So, what you are saying is that if you should be found here, we will face the same wrath because of hiding you that you face."

"That is the worst, but I am sure I will not be found here."

"I wish I was as confident about that as you make it sound."

"Besides, you have been and are well compensated for my being here, and I assure you that if push comes to shove I will disavow you having any knowledge of the real me."

"Easier said than done," Eileen interjected. "After all, situations can get so dangerous that the best of intentions can get tossed aside. Further, Tessie and Sal know all of this. Is there anyone else involved?"

"No. I swear to you this is it all."

"How can we get in touch with Tessie to get her slant on this? The secure telephone line I used in the past to talk to her has been abandoned."

"I am afraid there is no way. The only way we figured this could work is that all ties be broken completely. Of course, Tessie may show up at some point."

Grady was adamant. "Are you sure you are telling us everything?"

"Yes."

Eileen was noncommittal. "You must understand that we need to talk this over among ourselves. Our lives and this place can be in danger."

"No more so than if I was Tessie."

"Not quite," Grady said sternly. "Tessie, if that was the truth, was trying to protect Sal. You are the primary target of who knows what."

ELEVEN

When told of the deception, Cuba and Hilda showed no surprise. They had enough confidence in Grady to decide what, if anything, needed to be done differently and they would just go along with it. They had agreed among themselves that unless there was a direct threat to their well being they would stay the course no matter what. They were happy and it would take a major upheaval to change that.

In their private discussions, Grady and Eileen expressed a basic concern, but they decided, even if reluctantly, to let things coast along. As long as the monthly amount for Vicky kept coming in, they would wait and see. They had been running an account of how much Vicky's work efforts should be deducted from the monthly amount even though they had no way of communicating that. They surmised that somehow Vicky and Tessie were in touch with each other. They wondered what else Vicky was secretive about. That at least there were two other people out there who knew where Vicky was seemed to be a major weakness in her so-called disappearance. If, in fact, there were bad people after her, they would stop at nothing to find her. Grady and Eileen could not be sure if she was overstating or understating her posture. There was probably an incentive to do it either way.

The one direct effect for Grady was that Eileen's reasoning on his original idea made even more sense now. Compared to his actually partaking in the elimination of people, even if it was for a worthy cause, if he was fretting about the current situation he could only imagine the impact that would have had on his state of apprehension and thought patterns.

An uneventful month passed and things seemed to have settled to a point where they were lulled into a form of acceptance of the situation. Little did they know that an even larger surprise was ahead.

It was early Wednesday afternoon and the lunch period had just wound down. The tables had been cleared, the dishes washed, and Grady and Eileen had finished straightening out the dining room. They were headed back to their room to take a rest when they saw the woman standing by the front door with a large suitcase besides her. A guest was not registered for arrival so they approached her cautiously. "Can we help you?" Eileen's voice shook ever so slightly.

The voice sounded familiar. "Do you have a permanent room available?"

They moved closer to her. "Who are you?"

"I am glad you don't recognize me. My alteration is a success. I am Tessie."

As they moved closer, there were features that became recognizable. The posture and plumpness had been noted before. To be sure, Grady reached for her arm and pushed up the sleeve of the silk blouse. There was the scar on her wrist. "How did you get here?"

"In a way no one will ever know. And, since I have no way to go back, you are stuck with me. Love the addition, by the way."

Grady and Eileen looked at each other. Surprise was written all over their faces. Eileen spoke up. "What do you really want?"

"I still need to disappear. I also want to be with my sister. I want to be here. I want to be with you since I feel I can trust you. There will be double the monthly amount and you will still have more rooms available for other guests than there used to be."

"Let's step outside for a moment." Grady gestured to the door. Once outside, he continued. "I don't want anyone else to overhear our conversation. Are the same people after Vicky after you?"

"Maybe."

"Maybe?"

"She knows who is after her. They probably don't have the same purpose concerning Sal, but to be as honest as possible I am not sure."

"That's not very reassuring."

"Look, I know I am asking much from you, but you are being very well paid not to mention the addition now in place and paid for. If you are really uncomfortable with this I'll try to make other arrangements for me and my sister but there might wind up to be more danger than if we leave things as they are."

"What do you mean by that?"

"More outside contacts, more exposure, events and transactions most likely traceable to here."

"So," Eileen said with a touch of anger, "What you are saying is we really have no choice."

"I am sorry, but I will make it up to you. I'll be as helpful as possible and no trouble, I promise."

Grady muttered. "I think trouble is just beginning."

TWELVE

Another unexpected development for Cuba and Hilda to accept and move on with. The one thing Hilda knew for sure was that she would have to make more popovers.

Grady and Eileen decided they would have to be more careful about which guests could be let in. They would still only accept cash for the actual stay but would require a check for the deposit. That way there would at least be a checking account they could verify as needed. Perhaps that would not amount to much in this sophisticated cyber world, but it added a level of difficulty for evil motives.

Tessie announced she would be known as Jane Foresythe. Jane and Vicky ate their meals together in one of their rooms. They did not mingle with the guests, and each performed whatever tasks were asked of them. They were no trouble and did their part to be unnoticed. They stayed in their rooms or visited each other except when called upon to do work.

An uneventful autumn and winter passed. The Inn was usually filled, and there was only one week in January when there were no guests at all. Grady and Eileen were feeling more relaxed and that meant they could enjoy themselves in their enamored place. The beauty and solitude fed a spawning love.

Grady had thought so much about the fabricated story about the marsh that he told to Vicky that he decided it was worth treating it as if it was real. He built the railing for guests to lean against to peer out and ponder the mysteries of the marsh. Or, they could just sit in the ledge and take the entire expanse in. He created and embellished the story on a board that he affixed to the tree at the end of the railing. His determination to write a book using that as the background was fixed as well.

Spring brought an even greater influx of guests, and the marsh exhibit proved to be captivating for one and all. Guests talked about it, and they walked there numerous times proclaiming that on each sighting they saw something new. For those caring to go, Grady conducted a special walk to the marsh on moonlit nights and he would embellish the tale with some morbid details.

They should have been on guard knowing that things were going too well. It was on a Wednesday and the Inn was nearly full. Breakfast time was over and Vicky and Jane had not shown up. They usually went to the kitchen to get coffee and a danish to take back to one of their rooms to have a quiet time together. It was not like them to have skipped the meal.

Eileen went to Jane's room. She knocked twice and when there was no response she opened the unlocked door. Not only was there no Jane, there was no sign that she had ever been there. The bed was made up. All of the clothing and personal items were gone. Eileen checked the bathroom and all of the toiletries were missing. The place was wiped clean. It was the same situation at Vicky's room.

They did not know what to make of it. Both women were their usual selves the night before and appeared relaxed and amiable. Had they been snatched away by the forces they dreaded? There was no indication in either room of a struggle or an unwarranted intrusion. There was nothing on the film from the security cameras, and not even a glimpse of them leaving alone or with others. What could have changed? Why had they not said anything if plans had changed? Then there was the unnerving thought of what, if anything, they could do about it? It was not something they could turn to the police about. Contacting Sal might be a bad idea even if they knew where to reach him. An inner circle discussion concluded that there was nothing they could do at the moment. Hopefully, some explanation would be forthcoming.

Further mystification came at the end of the month when there was no deposit to the Inn's account for Jane and Vicky. Only Jane could stop that. Was she coerced to do it? Did that confirm that for whatever reason they had gone elsewhere? Did the offshore bank get notice that she was deceased?

The only upside was that they now had two additional rooms for guests. There were many repeat guests as well as guests staying for longer periods of time.

It was Wednesday morning when Grady passed the dining area headed for the kitchen. Ladson Allen was just finishing his breakfast. This was his third weekly stay, and after learning that he was a New York Times best seller author, Grady decided that when there was an opportunity he would approach him for some advice on the book he anticipated writing. This seemed as good a time as any as the author was the only person still in the dining area. Grady approached him and started to clear away the dishes. "Excuse me, Mr. Allen, when you have some time I would like to talk to you about a book I would like to write."

"Grady, please call me Ladson. I am asked that frequently and don't mind at all talking to you about it. How about meeting me just outside the front door in about twenty minutes. You can tag along on my morning walk to the marsh, a place that holds a particular fascination for me."

"Thanks. That would be fine."

Grady was waiting when Ladson came through the front door. As they started out, Ladson was the first to speak. "Your place here is a marvel. The time I spend here helps me write, not the writing as much as getting my mind in a creative mode. The peace and quiet does its thing. The marsh speaks to me. One might think my ideas would have dried up after writing twelve books, but they are refreshed here. There are not too many places that can do such a service. Thank you for doing this."

"I am glad it helps you. Many find solace and solutions here, and it even does it for me as well."

"So, what would you like to know about writing?"

"The marsh speaks to me as well. I was intrigued by that

place when I first surveyed the place. The story I posted there is what I would like to use as the background for a novel."

"Would be appealing to readers I am sure."

"To be frank, I don't know how to start it."

Ladson laughed. "You start by starting. It's as simple as that. I'll tell you a secret about writers. There are as many theories about writing as there are writers. Basically, you go with what works for you. I have run the gamut. Usually, I have no idea how a book will end. At times, I have a beginning, and at other times I have only a middle. The ending somehow develops seemingly on its own as the story develops. If at any point I am bogged down, I introduce a new character or use a diversionary device, such as a flashback. Start with what you think might be a beginning, and don't be surprised if it turns out to be the middle." They were at the marsh, and sat on the ledge. Ladson strained to peer out over the wavering grasses as if he wanted to hear all it was conveying to him. "I come here at night if there is a moon, and I can hear stories in the wind. This place is fascinating, and if you let yourself fall in with it the motivation to start will arise. It will surprise you how really easy it is."

"I hope so. When I first found what would become the Inn I was actually drawn more to the marsh and the cemetery."

"Fosters contemplation, an author's bonanza."

"Thank you for the advice and taking time to talk with me."

"I actually have an ulterior motive. I need to ask something from you."

"Oh?"

"The Inn of Endless Time has a uniqueness that can serve many purposes."

"I seem to be constantly learning that."

"Unless you know about it, unless you need it, just as I do to find my deep self, there are people that can be lost here."

Grady was hesitant to say more. "It appears to be so."

Ladson looked forlorn. He gazed out over the wind blown grasses and was silent. Grady thought he might have reconsidered saying anything and that this was the end of the discussion or that he was pondering what might be the best way to say what was on his mind. "I have what you may think is a strange request. First, it demands I tell you a story about myself. I have been successful and quite rich by most standards. There is much truth to the edict that success and wealth do not necessarily result in happiness. I have been a lonely man. Success and riches bring many acquaintances but nary a friend. I have never married. I have never loved any woman except one. And that is the story that often drives me to despair. When I was in high school, I deeply and earnestly loved an intelligent and vivacious girl. She loved me as well, and we spent wonderful and memorable times together. Cruelly, now that I look back on it, our parents thought we were too serious and managed to keep us apart. The relationship withered under the strain. My world crashed around me. There has never been anyone even close to the way I felt about her. That agony, while making me a deep writer, has left me an empty person." His voice choked up and a tear appeared at a corner of one eye and rolled down his cheek. "My moment was gone, but it may not be too late for others."

A long silence prompted Grady to inquire, "What do you mean?"

"History repeats itself." Ladson's voice was trembling and it took him a moment before he resumed speaking. "The details are painful, as if I was reliving my past. I will just tell you the gist of it. My niece is sixteen and in love with a boy, also sixteen. They are serious, bright, and mature. In every sense they know what they are about and what they are doing. As far as I can tell, their love is the real thing. My brother and his wife, shades of my past, have forbidden her to see him anymore. The boy has a single mother who is spiteful of the relationship. The youngsters come to me constantly for advice, and are so desperate to be together they have contemplated a pregnancy. I convinced them that would not be the thing to do. I have promised to help them. The more time that I spend here, this would be the perfect place for them. They love nature. They are good and responsible, and they can help around here. I will pay for their permanent stay. You can claim that all you know is that you hired a young married couple to work the Inn. They can pass for older people. No one will find them here, I am sure. It is a way for them to be together and to give their love a chance to survive, a chance I never had."

Ladson buried his face in his hands. Grady was sure the man was agonizing over this dilemma. Grady did not know what to say, although he knew he would have to talk to Eileen, Cuba, and Hilda. "I feel for your pain and respect your wanting to help. I am not sure this would be a solution, but I will talk it over with all of my folks here."

"Thank you, Grady."

The marsh heard it all. A sharp wind blew the grasses and a low eerie sound, much like whining, surrounded them. They walked slowly back to the Inn and nothing further was said.

THIRTEEN

Grady pretty well predicted Eileen's reaction. "Here we go, again!"

In line with the humor she was trying to instill in him, he tried to be jovial. "Maybe, we should change the name of the Inn to Inn Trouble, Inn One-Way or Inn Trouble, Inn Visible."

She smiled at his attempt to lessen the impact of the new situation. "Maybe, we should make ourselves disappear instead."

"It might be the easy way out."

"Life is complicated. Perhaps, all things related to it are also complicated."

"I have already told Cuba and Hilda that there will be a conference after dinner."

"Good. None of us are parents, however, so I am not sure we can fully relate to that point-of-view."

It was becoming a familiar scene as they gathered in the kitchen after all of the dinner tasks were completed. Grady repeated the request and background that Ladson had urged. "Well, that's it," he said stoically. "In a sense we have been here and done that. Only the names and the faces will have changed."

"Not quite," Eileen interjected. "The ladies, as far as we know, were trying to escape from evil, supposedly a life and death situation. Even in theory, this is not the same. Where do we draw the line? Can, or more appropriately, should we rightfully interfere in the destiny of people?"

"For which I might add," Grady asserted, "We will be paid

in full."

"So, you are saying if we get paid for it we should do it?"

"Not if we are not comfortable with it. That was your argument against the elimination prospect. Losing people is a different ballgame. Speak your mind folks so we can decide whether this is a go or not."

Eileen was the first to speak. "I have already touched on this when Grady told me about this earlier today. We are not parents and can only guess what parental emotions and practicalities may be involved in such a situation. The motivation might be good here, but all sorts of misinterpretations might arise. For instance, we can easily be considered as kidnappers."

Grady interrupted, "But, we would not have brought them here, and they would not be held by force or without their consent."

Eileen retorted, "I am not sure a minor can give consent, especially to a situation such as this. I think we need to revisit the basic provision. We should not go under the assumption that anyone who seeks escape or shelter here from the outside world will not be found. Slip ups and other mistakes can happen, particularly it would seem with young people. What if they contact their friends?"

This time Grady waited until she was finished speaking. "Even if they are found, Ladson assures me they look older than they are, and we can assert that we hired them to work here and took them at their word they were over age and even married."

"Are we that good at lying?"

"We'll have to be. Hilda, what do you think?"

Hilda glanced at Cuba. "As with everything else, it is up to the two of you to decide. Again, we appreciate you letting us in on it all but it affects you more than us. We could always use some more help in the kitchen if that arises but we will do whatever needs to be done."

Cuba nodded. "We speak as one."

"It might be a refreshing change to have some young folks around," Hilda added.

Grady smiled. "Eileen and I are too old, eh?"

Hilda had a deep laugh. "You know that is not what I meant."

"I know. Perhaps, you are right though. Young blood might help us all."

Eileen smiled. "I am not sure I like your choice of words. But, to be serious about this, I assume then that we all approve of this latest adventure. Yet, it has to be on the condition that Ladson will take them away if for any reason we say it is not working out."

The next day Grady informed Ladson about going forward with the plan under the stated condition. He thought that was reasonable, and he indicated it might be a couple of weeks before he could work things out at his end. He would give them advance notice when it all came together.

That night as they lay in bed, a shudder went through Eileen. There was too much uncertainty here for her liking, and she was not totally convinced this was the right thing to do. Grady sensed her uneasiness and held her tightly. Worrying was not going to help, although worrying was part and parcel of the risk.

FOURTEEN

A cold misting rain fell from a gray laden sky. By all accounts, it was a nasty day. It certainly was not inviting for one to venture outdoors, but Grady was on a mission. After the breakfast time, with raincoat, rain hat, and boots, he set out for the marsh. He tried to convince himself it was to garner inspiration for writing the book, but he knew the true goal was to bridge the gap between the story he conjured up about the marsh and the true mysteries lurking in the deep.

He was surprised when he arrived at the destination that he was not alone there. Lillian Shaster was perched on the seating ledge, umbrella in hand, peering out over the fog-shrouded grasses. A widow and retired school teacher, Lillian Shaster was a repeat guest at the Inn. She would stay only two or three days at a time, and other than showing up at the meals she enjoyed so much, she was rarely seen except for an occasional visit to the book nook. Grady guessed she was in her seventies, overweight as an offshoot from the food she enjoyed so much, and if she cared to look at you at all the piercing brown eyes below graying bangs told you she would tolerate no nonsense. She must have ruled her classroom with stern looks and a lack of tolerance for errant behavior.

"I did not expect anyone to be here," Grady said softly as she turned to look at his intrusion. "Mrs. Shaster, you should not be out on a day like this."

"I did not expect another soul to be here today, Mr. Oslow." Her voice was as sharp as her glances. "I take great solace in this spot."

"So do I, Mrs. Shaster."

"I am at an age when feelings can be misleading, but when I am here I feel sensations that remind me of my youth. It forces me to remember things I have long since blocked from my mind."

"Solitude can be a wonderful thing."

"Not always."

"No, not always."

"Mr. Oslow, since my Peter died four years ago, I have been a lonely woman. I miss him terribly. I did not appreciate him enough when I had him and all the things, little and big, that he did for me. I would give anything to have him yell at me for keeping the heat too high."

"How long were you married?"

"Forty-eight years."

"Wow! A tribute to a solid relationship. How did you meet?"

"At our town's July 4th picnic. It was a moment I cannot forget. How did you meet your wife?"

"Here, at the Inn. I am an ole buzzard, but we are newlyweds."

"Good for you.."

"I can see you like your privacy. I will leave you alone just as long as you promise not to stay out too long in this bad weather."

"No, please, stay awhile. My loneliness is overwhelming, and it is good to talk with you."

Grady sat next to her on the ledge. "May I call you Lillian?"

"Yes."

"Call me, Grady."

"Alright."

A few minutes of silence passed. She turned to him, and there were tears in her eyes. "I want to be with my Peter."

Grady swallowed hard and hoped she did not mean what he was hearing. "You will some day."

She wept openly. "I cannot wait until then. I want to walk

out in the marsh and die there."

"Lillian, there are people I am sure who want you to go on, and there must be things that remain undone."

She spoke between sobs coming from deep within her. "Not really. Material things have always been unimportant to me. We did not have any children. My dearest friend died a year ago, and there is no one I want to see or to be with. My will leaves everything to charity."

"On a sunny day, you will feel better about everything."

"I come here on sunny days, and I feel the same way. I am determined to do this. My problem is I am afraid. I cannot do it by myself."

He was quiet for a moment. "Your fear is telling you it is something you should not do."

"No. Basically, I am a weak woman. I often had to lean on Peter to get things done. Please take my hand, walk me out there and then just leave me."

"Lillian, I can't do that. Let's talk some more. I am sure there are things that we can find to give you the will to go on."

"This is not a rash decision. God understands and will forgive me. I have left a note in the room explaining this."

"Is there a minister or priest you can talk this over with?"

"No."

"How about your doctor?"

"No."

"There are other alternatives. I will talk to my wife, and I am sure we can find a place here with us. Perhaps, you can be in charge of the book nook."

"Grady, you are a sweet and kind man, just like my Peter. It just makes me want to be with him that much more."

All sorts of thoughts went through Grady's mind. All of the years when the concept of eliminating certain people was rational and justifiable, and now he balked at an act which would mercifully end this woman's misery. She was not asking him to kill her, just to hold her hand. Did he have the right to deny her that assistance? He watched her intent stare outward to the place she felt Peter was waiting for her. He knew if he did not do this now, he would never be able to do it. He reached for her hand. Her brittle fingers were very cold. He stood and pulled her up and they walked into the marsh. He doubted if she even noticed the cold, soggy underfooting. At places they sank in over their ankles. Water and mud spilled over the top of his boots. Lillian stumbled a few times and leaned against him for support and it was all he could do to keep her from falling. He could no longer see the seating area they had left behind. They reached a slight mound in the marsh, and she turned to him. Her voice was raspy, barely audible over the wind and whining grasses. "This is far enough. Leave me. Thank you for your kind act." She leaned towards him and cracked lips kissed him on the cheek. "Go. Please leave me." As if he was her pupil and had completed the assignment he turned and headed back. He dared not turn around to look at her as he trodded back oblivious to the cold, the wetness, the mud, and snakes that were undoubtedly tracking his path.

Back at the ledge, he peered out over the engulfing vastness, and it was all a blur. He could not see her, and he cried. The sadness of it all hung over him heavily. After a long period of time, as if he was waiting for her to reappear, he went back to the Inn. There was no way for him to decide whether he had done good or ill. He just had to accept his participation in what was a special and meaningful act for a lonely old woman.

Back at the Inn, he realized he was caked in mud from the knees down. Even the bottom part of his raincoat was mud laden. He hosed himself off with the outside hose, leaving the boots, the raincoat, and his socks on the bench by the utility shed. He dried himself off with a rag from the pile in the shed.

Grady cried again as he went to Lillian's room and read the note she had left there. The note was attached to her Last Will and Testament.

My Peter is calling me from the marsh.
I am going to join him. Do not be sad
for me.

Lillian Shaster

Eileen detected the pain in his voice and the shuddering of his body as she held him. There was no way she could judge what he had done or even guess at what she might have done if it had been her and not Grady.

The County Sheriff was notified. He assembled a group of men, including dogs, and they fanned out in the marsh. They went all the way to the river. No sign of Lillian was found, not even her umbrella. The case was closed. Lillian had found her endless time.

FIFTEEN

She had always been serious minded, and throughout her young life being so serious had made things difficult for Cassidy Knowles. Other youngsters shied away from her, and adults were quick to describe her as weird. Books were her only friends, the only things she felt comfortable with. The out-of-doors, away from snickering children and adults looking at her with disapproval, was her refuge. Walks in the woods were far more satisfying than electronic gadgets. The expectations of her parents and the dictates of society were alien to her. Uncle Ladson was the only adult who had any inkling of who she was and what she was about. He reassured her many times that there was nothing wrong with her and that it was the rest of the world that was awry. That comforted her and emboldened her to be different despite the consequences.

On her third day in high school, Cassidy saw Ethan Zilber sitting by himself in the library. One look into those hazel eyes told her that he was a kindred spirit. The book on the table before him on nature confirmed her first impression. She sat across from him and his smile said all she needed to hear. His overly protective mother had shielded him from most ordinary happenings but was no impediment to a love that was borne from the extraordinary.

For two years there was little intrusion into their world. Parents and peers thought little of the pair and their togetherness, and any conclusion was premised on strange behavior by a couple of disassociated youngsters. Forced psychiatric analysis confirmed wayward and unhealthy behavior spawned from unconventional attitudes. A total separation of the couple was the avowed remedy.

The adult world underestimated the true nature of the two individuals and the essence of their love. Superior intelligence furthered all sorts of creative plans to stay together. Uncle Ladson, sympathetic to their plight, would be the key to the most viable option. When he proposed to them that he could effectuate their disappearance at the Inn of Endless Time, they knew their world was righted. It reinforced the notion that all things are possible with determination and a little help.

A cryptic note was left behind which merely stated that their love was for real and they had run away and nobody should bother to look for them. They would be together and safe.

For several weeks the couple had secreted clothing and personal items to Ladson's house. They were in his car when he picked them up at the prearranged desolate spot for the trip to the Inn. It was a special magical beginning for them. For Ladson, it was a form of redemption.

Grady and Eileen had little experience with children or teenagers, but they were both struck by how mature the two youngsters were. They looked older than their years, and conversations were easily on an adult level. There was no doubt they were in love. Eileen could relate to how they held hands as much as possible, and there was the intent look at one another which can only be based on deep affection.

Ladson left after the pair was settled in. Initially, they would be helping in the kitchen, and Cuba would keep them in line if that became necessary. Neither knew anything about the workings of a kitchen, but they were quick and enthusiastic learners. Since they loved nature, Grady also intended to use their help in maintaining the trails and other outside chores. The first time he took them to the marsh, he could tell they were spellbound by the site as well as the alleged tale behind it. Grady did not have the heart to tell them he had made up the story. After all, it has been known that some stories take on a life of their own.

After a couple of weeks, it seemed as if the young couple had been with them for a long time. The youngsters were pleasant and cooperative, and they made no demands whatsoever. Whenever they were not doing tasks, they walked the trails and stayed at the marsh for long periods of time. It was as if that magical place understood their plight. If only the rest of the world could be as accommodating. In the evenings, they were often in the book nook reading.

Ladson reported that the police had been notified of the disappearance of the children. He had been questioned and his far-reaching author's mind had created a story that convinced the authorities of his detachment from the situation. His initial observation was that while the parents feigned overt concern they were basically relieved that they did not have to deal with any fractured situation. For those who do not want or know how to handle a problem, if the problem is removed it is in a sense a form of resolution.

Cuba and Hilda especially enjoyed having the youngsters in the kitchen. Their playful mannerism and keen interest in learning all facets of food preparation made for engrossing moments. Cassidy, who asked to be called Cassie, was particularly swept up in making desserts, and that endeared her to Hilda.

One night as Eileen stroked Grady's arm, she whispered wistfully, "I can see now how much I may have missed not having children."

Grady embraced her tightly. "It does add a further dimension to life. Yet, we can, at least, have some of that with their presence in our lives."

"You are right, and it is fruitless to regret what cannot be changed. Too bad we did not meet when we were young. Our love children would have been fulfilling."

"No doubt."

"I am content having you now."

"I feel the same way about you. Our timing may not have been the best but it does not detract from what we have now."

"You are a keeper, innkeeper."

“You are a keeper, innkeeper.”
An echo of love.

SIXTEEN

Peaceful weeks passed for the folks at the Inn Endless Time. Cassie and Ethan probably enjoyed the time more than the others. They had finally found the peace in which their love could flourish. When not working or reading, they would walk the trails and linger for long periods at the marsh. They were drawn to the shrouded mystery of the place, and it represented a symbol to them of a dream-based escape from a world ever set against them being together. That unreasonable stance was also a mystery to them.

When there was a full moon, they also went to the marsh. The added aura of intrigue seemed most appropriate. On one such occasion, Ethan stroked Cassie's arm through her sweater. "I wonder, Cass, how long our luck will hold out. It is wonderful here, and the people have been awfully good to us. I would hate for them to get into any trouble on account of us."

Cassie turned to him, and in the moonlight his eyes appeared even larger than they were. "They know the risk, and so do we. I love them and I love this place, our place. Let's hope this is forever, and if it turns out not to be we'll come here to the marsh and follow the young girls to our forever."

"Just as a last resort. We have so much living to do, and I want our love to be an inspiration to others."

"Of course. Uncle Ladson will help us again if we need him. Why can't all adults be like him and our Inn family?"

"I have no answer to that. We live in a precarious world where there is hate when there should be love and selfishness and greed when there should be sharing. All the more reason we need to hold ourselves out as role models."

Cassie lightly touched his cheek. "I'll never understand how the world can be so intolerant of two people who find their own private world within the bigger world."

"Me neither, but at this point it makes no difference. We have our world so let's just live in it as we want to."

"I am still shocked by my mom's reaction when she asked me how I know that I love you. I told her about all the things we share, and even if she was listening it did not register with her. When I told her that I can tell what you are thinking by the way you touch me, she actually laughed. Poor woman has evidently never experienced a sensation that makes all things beautiful and meaningful. I guess the most puzzling aspect is how can a person who knows nothing about love be able to judge that one who is in love is not really in love?"

"I had the same bout with my parents. I told them it is not something you can adequately explain since it is a feeling, a knowing that when two hearts touch it is the path to the future."

"I love you with all my heart."

"I love you with all my heart and then some."

"I love you even when you are silly. As long as there is a full moon let's go to the graveyard. Those adults don't deny our love."

"They are not all adults. People back then did not live as long as people do today, and by the dates there are some there that are younger than we are when they died."

"I wonder if any of them were in love as we are. How many died from a broken heart?"

"We can only imagine. We are not the first youngsters to be in love."

"And we won't be the last, thank goodness."

"That is why we have to make this last."

"That is a given. I can't ever imagine being without you."

"You never will be."

"Promise me that."

"I promise."

At the cemetery, they counted the headstones. There were 117, and as lovers they designated that number as a secret code if they ever needed one. Not trusting the outside world leads to all sorts of contingency planning.

Hand-in-hand they walked slowly back to the Inn. Once in their room they played their favorite game of undressing each other. In the shower, their bodies molded together as if the cascading water was a mystical glue. A familiar touch, a familiar kiss, familiar yet brimming with a freshness that constantly reinforced their private feelings.

Later in a sleep clutching at one another, there seemed to be nothing now that could challenge their oneness. Each moment was in endless time.

SEVENTEEN

Eileen shuddered when she saw in the pile of mail a plain manila envelope with no return address and the Inn Endless Time address in large block print. There was a Chicago postmark. The envelope was not bulky, and it might even be empty. In any event, it appeared ominous and she hesitated in opening it.

Inside was an article cut out from a Chicago newspaper. It was brief but made Eileen tremble even more. Two female bodies had been discovered in an abandoned house, both so badly burned that the police doubted their identities could ever be established. She had a good idea who they were, but who had sent the article? More to the point, why was it sent?

Eileen went immediately to Grady to show him the article. His reaction was the same, and he further thought they would probably hear more from the source. Was it just a notification or was it a warning? Even if this was the end of the story, what had happened along the way? It was still puzzling why the ladies had left the Inn, even if willingly. How did they leave? Where did they go? The newspaper article in a way raised more questions than answers. Perhaps that was the intent, to torment them.

Cuba and Hilda shook their heads in disbelief at the news. It all seemed so far removed from their world that it raised little concern, although they knew they could not be completely complacent about it. There was no point in telling Cassie and Ethan about any of this as their world was already in flux.

The more they thought about it, the more troubling the

significance of the article became. Whoever sent it must have considered a connection between them and the ladies. What could that portend?

After further thought and discussion, it was decided that worrying about it all was counterproductive and that they would just continue being cautious with all people and all actions. There certainly were enough things going on to keep them somewhat distracted.

That determination came into sharp focus the next day when an unannounced visitor showed up at the Inn. When Eileen opened the front door after hearing the knock, she was greeted by a middle-aged man, short and stocky with a well-trimmed beard. His voice was cultured. "My name is James Havill. I wonder if I might have a tour of the place?"

With suspicions already in full swing, Eileen's guard was up. Her voice was unusually tentative. "Are you considering a stay?"

"For sure." His smile seemed genuine.

Eileen showed him around and let him see a room that was at the moment unoccupied. She gave him a map of the trails. He studied it for a few seconds. "Would you mind if I walk to the marsh?" His voice was pleasant, nearly mesmerizing.

"That will be fine. I'll be here when you get back if you want to make a reservation. If you do, I'll need to see some identification and you need to fill out some paper work."

An hour later he was back. "Let me give you my card. That will explain a good bit."

The card read:

JAMES HAVILL
President
National Right to Die League
712 Conway Concourse
Vestal, New Hampshire

Eileen held the card gingerly. "It tells me who you are, but does not clarify your reason for being here."

He pointed to the book nook. "Can we sit over there?"

After sitting, he continued slowly. "The story of the suicide here I doubt made the national papers, but since I live only an hour away it did make the local paper, especially since the sheriff amassed such a large search party to look for and failed to find the body. As you probably know, it is against the law in this state and nearly all others to enable a person to exercise their right to die. My organization attempts to grant that privilege whenever possible. Of course, when people are terminal and bedridden, there is little we can do except to find a sympathetic doctor who might chance easing the way. Yet, there are times when a person is still mobile and completely rational and who seeks a place and moment of peace to effectuate the wish to end any suffering and torment. I suspected this would be such a place, and my visit here has confirmed that. The marsh is a magical place. It can hide secrets. I had gathered from the story that the woman had picked this place for that reason. I can see that a person can be at peace here for a time before and during their personal choice. I assure you that your price will be paid, that you will have no actual involvement in actions taken, there will be no fanfare, and all will be private and discreet."

Eileen interrupted him. "Mr. Havill, we are in the business to make people happy, including ourselves. We do not want to see or have people die here."

"You will be doing a very good deed, and there can be great satisfaction and comfort in fulfilling a person's final wish. When you think about it, such is a form of happiness."

"Stay for a moment. I am going to get my husband. I am sure he can tell you better than I can that this is a place of life and not death."

Eileen returned with Grady and James repeated his scenario. He added, "I do not expect an immediate answer. It does require a commitment and prolonged thought is best. We are not talking about a flood of cases here. It will not be too many, and besides yourselves only me and the person involved will know they have been here and what has happened."

After James left, Eileen suggested they take a walk. It was a few minutes before she spoke, knowing that whatever she was going to say only Grady could hear it. "I can't believe that at one time I was shocked at your scheme for prompting death for certain people. Now, it seems, that death is becoming an integral part of our business. I suppose I identify with the problem James faces. My mother died only after a long period of suffering. I was at a loss what to do about it, and I know she would have consented if there was a way to ease the situation. I guess what I am trying to say is that in any success there are probably burdens, maybe even self-imposed, that alter the pathway. You started with that premise, and I now see it head on. If James can pull off his end, I think we should do this."

Grady reached for her hand and grasped it firmly. "Each day I realize that my greatest luck and joy is in having you. You are a magnificent person. I envision this as a touchy situation, not quite as clear cut as James makes it out to be. It would not be for the money, but as with Lillian there are other rewards."

They stopped at the marsh, gazing out into what was proving to be an abyss. The mysteries shrouded in this place accentuated the mysteries of the series of events now a major force in their lives. There had been no way of knowing when the venture began that there might be forces encountered not strictly within their control. How many would prove to be sinister was the unknown.

EIGHTEEN

An uneventful three weeks passed. Nothing further on the Chicago bodies. No alerts from Ladson to upset Cassie and Ethan. Nothing from James, although he had telephoned twice to thank them for their assisting decision. Grady and Eileen were constantly on edge. It was as if they were waiting for the other shoe to drop.

Grady and Eileen had talked on many occasions just how fortunate they were not only to have each other and this wonderful place, but that they also had good physical and mental health. A peak appreciation is further enhanced when one comes across another person who is not so lucky. So, when James telephoned to inform them that he would be bringing Jessica Yarrow to the Inn the following week, Jessica's story tugged at their hearts. Jessica had been born deaf and with a debilitating physical deformity. A valiant heart and spirit as well as high intelligence led her to a life of bare contentment at an institution after her parents gave up trying to care for her. Now, at age thirty-two, Jessica was slowly becoming blind, and this was a crushing prospect for one even with vast courage. While her vision was not yet totally gone, she had contacted James with a wish to terminate her life before she was completely helpless. Medical recourse was not an option. Grady and Eileen knew this new involvement would not be easy, and it was already manifesting that kind of prospect.

When the other Inn folks were advised of Jessica's arrival, Cassie openly wept. She asked if she might personally look after Jessica for her stay. They already knew about her caring nature so it was agreed to. Eileen expressed some concern that she might be too young to be so close to a sudden life to death transition, but there was no denying the young woman's desire. One is probably never too young to learn about the possible harsh intricacies of human nature.

It was Tuesday afternoon when James drove in at the Inn with Jessica. Jessica was short, slightly plump, and had thin brown hair cut just below her ears. She leaned visibly to the left and a short deformed left arm was noticeable even beneath the sweater she was wearing. Sunglasses most likely were a form of protection for failing sight. She was mobile enough to get out of the car by herself. Cassie ran to her and hugged her, and Jessica tentatively put her good right arm around the girl who had surprised her with a show of emotion. Adept at lip reading as long as her sight held out, she thanked the young woman for the robust greeting and asked her to call her Jessie. Cassie told her to call her Cassie. Grady carried the small suitcase when they took Jessie to her room, and Cassie stayed with her to help get her settled.

"I never knew that doing good can make one sad," Eileen said huskily as she grasped Grady's arm. "I am not sure I can get used to this."

"You're not supposed to get used to it. Just think of it as supplying the setting to allow one to do what they want. We need to find satisfaction in that."

"I can already tell this will be especially hard for Cass."

"People who feel deeply do not have an easy road to travel on."

"We need to be here for her, too."

"We will. Ethan is her bedrock just as you are mine."

It did not take long for all of them to confirm that Jessie was a strong woman. She had to be for all she had gone through and was still going through. Around each bend in her life travel was yet another challenge, another adversity to overcome. When the doctors told her that there was no way that her eyesight could be saved, an end to the only sensation she had left fostered the resolve to end the hardship before there was nothing left. Yet, after a few days at the Inn, she discovered a sensation she thought she did not have. The attention and caring of a young woman seeped into her heart and she discovered the feeling of love. Cassie spoke to her constantly and caringly, and Jessie sensed the genuine sympathy the youngster had for her plight. Even in fading eyesight, fleeting images revealed that Cassie was a beautiful person inside and out. For all of her setbacks, it brought a certain contentment that her final days were so imbued with this kind of experience.

On the fourth day of her stay, Jessie told James she was ready. She asked for a private moment with Cassie, and she hugged the young woman with all of the strength her good right arm was capable of. "Dearest child," she uttered as she felt Cassie sobbing, "Do not be sad for me. This is my choice, a victory as I see it. You have made my final days happy, so I am fortified by your kindness. Share your goodness with others. That is your calling. After all, you are an angel."

Cassie wept openly as she held Jessie's hand as they made their way slowly to the marsh. Grady, James, and Ethan followed closely behind.

When they reached the marsh, Jessie kissed Cassie on the forehead and then hugged the other three. Grady held her firmly around the waist as he guided her into the marsh. Cassie cried in Ethan's arms as James looked on pensively. In a few minutes they could no longer see the pair. Only Cassie's relentless sobs broke the silence.

It seemed like an eternity before Grady returned to the landing. He nodded to the group and they returned to the Inn without exchanging a word. Ethan supported Cassie's whimpering body the entire way and they went right to their room when they entered the Inn. James had already packed his things and he had Jessie's suitcase as well, and he left after paying the bill. His handshake to Grady and Eileen was firm. "Thank you again for this. It is a gentle act of humanity and makes us all better people."

Grady and Eileen walked to the marsh. A mist had settled over the area and nothing moved. The tall grasses were stationery and not a single bird could be seen or heard. In the significant quietness they kissed. Then they sat without speaking. At times, thoughts need not be expressed. Hand-in-hand they returned to the Inn, back to a different kind of reality.

NINETEEN

It was less than three weeks when James telephoned to arrange for the arrival of another candidate. He was quite apologetic about the short duration for this new one, and explained it was highly unusual for such a short interval. The next one might be many months off.

Professor Frank Markel, even at age ninety-three, was still a remarkable man. He had earned a doctorate of Philosophy at age eighteen and had taught at universities around the world, retiring at age eighty-seven after twenty-three years at Blantyre University. His publications spanned the entire teaching career and numbered in the hundreds. Some twenty years earlier, one of his graduate students had undertaken a survey of how many times his writings and ideas had been cited by others. He had documented over twenty thousand instances and was forced to admit that the survey was not exhaustive and probably never could be. The Professor still was writing, and remained critical of others who supported worn out doctrines and staid theories. When he was diagnosed with pancreatic cancer, he knew all too well what that meant. He refused any kind of treatment other than medicine to ease the pain. His wife, Gladys, had died many years earlier from liver cancer and he still shook his head in disbelief at the things she had to endure as he had to helplessly watch the onset of the inevitable. He contacted James, and when told of Inn Endless Time, Frank knew he wanted to spend a period of time at such a place before he effectuated his own peace.

The Professor had expected the place to be what it offered it to be, but he did not anticipate to be surrounded by such caring people, particularly a young woman named Cassie who affectionately understood his needs. For a week, the young woman barely left him and they even shared the glorious meals together. The best part was the long talks they had. She hung on his thoughts, and her interest in knowing and understanding was as genuine as his best students over the years.

At his request, one moonlit night Cassie took him to the marsh. They sat on the ledge, and she held his hand untroubled by the calloused skin. In the moonlight he saw a tear roll down her cheek. "Don't cry for me, child," he said in nearly a whisper. "Although I never expected anyone would. I lost my wife a long time ago. Our one son was killed in a motorcycle accident when he was twenty-two. One of the saddest facets of an already fragile life is to lose a child. We never could get over it fully. We could not ever talk about it, although that might have been the best thing to do. So, I have no one close to me, and then you came along in my closing days to share a kind and gentle time. I am very appreciative. How can I thank you?"

Cassie leaned over and kissed his stubbled cheek. "You don't have to thank me. I only wish to ease your pain and to give you a breath of love to hang on to."

He felt a tear roll down his cheek. "I suppose I should be grateful that I have lived as long as I have. I have met many people, experienced all sorts of emotions and feelings. Nothing is stronger than love, and for all of the theories and concepts of living life to its fullest, love is the greatest mystery because it can be complex and simple at the same time. When one is old, especially on the threshold of death, a long look back is not only appropriate, it is required. In spite of numerous good things a person may have done, any wrong can be haunting. When I was about your age a vivacious young girl, and you remind me so much of her, admired me because she thought I was so smart. Too smart for my own good was what I was. Intelligence can be its own worst enemy. I did not realize or understand or even appreciate how deeply she loved me. Cruelly,

I kept devising tests to see just how much she would do for me. I put her mercilessly through many an ordeal. A growing feeling on her part of constantly failing me, and not realizing or understanding what I was actually doing to her, she took her own life in a ghastly manner. That left a permanent scar on my heart. I swore I would never drive anyone else to the brink of their tolerance. Throughout my teaching years, I would let up often on students on the strict demands that true scholarship required. I wish I could apologize to her."

Cassie stroked his arm through the jacket he was wearing to ward off the evening chill. "What was her name?"

He did not answer right away, and she sensed his mind was a long way off. "Cheryl."

"Why don't you pretend I am Cheryl and you now have a second chance to say something to me?"

It is not easy for an old person to weep. His tears flowed as they used to when he was a young man and watched his parents being buried. He knew this wonderful young woman was giving him an opportunity to lessen the guilt that had plagued him for so many years. "Cheryl," his voice choking up, "Please forgive me for all the things I did, for all that I put you through. I did not want or mean to hurt you. I should have respected your feelings for me and protected you from my meanness. I am sorry, so sorry."

Cassie hugged him tightly. "I forgive you."

They sat in silence as a fog rolled in over the marsh. He knew he was ready.

Two days later, Grady led Frank into the marsh as James, Cassie, and Ethan looked on. Cassie's crying was the only sound piercing the eery stillness.

TWENTY

As luck would have it, the winter was the harshest in over a quarter of a century. The Inn remained empty as the county could not keep up with snow removal on the remote sections. The loss of income was offset by a certain emotional inertia that contributed to a relaxing and close time together for the residents. Cuba and Hilda spent enjoyable times teaching Cassie and Ethan some of the basics about preparing meals and desserts. In fact, one evening the youngsters made a complete dinner for all and it turned out most satisfactory with a warm and jovial time in the imbibing. The young couple not only quickly caught on to the knack of kitchen success, they loved doing it. That all promised to give Cuba and Hilda more help in the kitchen and with some extra time off. Grady and Eileen kept telling themselves that if guests could not make it to the Inn nobody else could either.

Then one interesting development occurred. On a day when the mailman could get through, he had over two weeks worth of mail for the Inn. One seemingly ominous letter with no return address and an El Paso, Texas postmark proved to be an eye-opener. It was typewritten and in all capital letters.

TO THE INNKEEPERS –

I DON'T DARE CALL, BUT I AM SURE YOU ARE ANXIOUS TO KNOW WHAT HAPPENED. WE RECEIVED A SECRET URGENT MESSAGE FROM SAL THAT IT WAS

KNOWN WE WERE AT THE INN. HE WAS ON HIS WAY TO PICK US UP HIMSELF. THERE WAS NO TIME FOR EXPLANATIONS. WE PACKED UP AND HE TOOK US TO A SECRET HIDING PLACE. WE KEEP MOVING FROM PLACE TO PLACE. IT IS A STRESSFUL WAY TO LIVE BUT NECESSARY.

SAL ARRANGED FOR TWO BODIES TO BE BURNED IN A DESERTED CHICAGO HOUSE TO THROW OTHERS OFF OUR TRAIL. SAL SENT YOU A COPY OF THE ARTICLE THINKING IT MIGHT ALSO SET YOUR MINDS TO REST. BELIEVE ME, YOU DON'T WANT TO KNOW WHERE HE GOT THE BODIES.

ANYWAY, I HAD TO STOP PAYMENTS TO THE INN BECAUSE HE THINKS THAT WAS COMPROMISED. SORRY, BUT I FIGURE YOU HAVE THE ANNEX SO YOU HAVE BEEN WELL PAID FOR ALL YOU DID. I ALSO THANK YOU GREATLY THAT YOU TOOK US IN AND TREATED US SO WELL. I WOULD HAVE BEEN MUCH HAPPIER IF THINGS HAD JUST GONE ON, BUT I NEED NOT TELL YOU THAT THINGS DON'T ALWAYS WORK OUT AS WE PLAN. IN ANOTHER LIFE.......MAYBE!

ANYWAY, I HOPE THE INN DOES WELL. NOW THAT WE ARE NOT THERE I DON'T THINK YOU ARE IN DANGER. YOU DON'T KNOW ANYTHING ANYWAY. THAT IS FOR THE BEST.

JANE

"I still wonder what kind of trouble Vicky was in for all of these drastic measures. I am of a mind we will never know." Eileen's voice trailed off along with the thought.

Grady added quickly, "As said, there are things we are better off not knowing. Sure is mysterious, though, and if I can I might work a variation of it in the book about the marsh if I can make it somewhat plausible. The real situation doesn't fully make any sense because we are stumbling around in the dark. Speaking of dark, one thing I do know is that I would not want to run into Sal in a dark alley."

"At least," Eileen offered with a laugh, "One of the problems is off our plate."

"The plate is still full."

"I know."

TWENTY-ONE

Many quirks exist in nature. One occurred as winter ended abruptly and spring emerged with gusto. One day, the Inn grounds were covered with ice and snow, and the next day it all melted and a bright warm sun engulfed the countryside. The telephone was busy with people seeking to make reservations. James also called to say he would be bringing two sisters at the same time the following week and they could share a room. Grady and Eileen looked at each other. "It couldn't be!"

Doreen Williams and Colleen Gertz were twin sisters. They were eighty-six years old, and each had lost a husband many years ago. They had married relatively late in life to older men and there were no children. They lived together in a senior apartment complex near Hartford, Connecticut. With a host of bodily lapses, Doreen was terminal. Colleen was physically well off but in an advanced stage of Alzheimer's. Doreen made the fateful decision for them to go together. She had voiced the memory of when they were little girls and they had expressed the wish that they would never want to go on without the other.

A few days before James was to bring the sisters to the Inn, Ladson telephoned from a public booth. He advised that although the parents were still not completely earnest in locating the youngsters, pressure from the authorities concerning such matters as education and a challenge from the Internal Revenue Service for them claiming the children as tax deductions, they had hired a private detective to find them. Ladson was under suspicion of being involved, and he was sure he was being followed and that his home telephone was tapped.

When Cassie and Ethan were told of this latest development, their mature reasoning which had now discarded any notion of a trip to the marsh especially in light of the marsh activity for James, their complete trust in Grady and Eileen led to a new plan. They would both be eighteen within a few months. They could legally get married in their own right, and while they would miss their Inn family who they had grown to love, they could be self sufficient anywhere with the increasing culinary skills they were learning. The plan would be, after the older people were let in on their secret code of 117 to match the number of headstones in the cemetery, if that number was conveyed orally or in writing, they would meet at Eileen's car and be taken to James' house until further movement was set in place. They were all sure that James would agree to this for all they were doing for him. In the meantime, Cassie and Ethan packed essentials and some clothing which was stored in the trunk of the car.

As anticipated, Cassie endeared herself to the sisters, and the pair spent two relaxing days before the trip to the marsh. Doreen, sensing the youngster's caring nature, opened up to her about many personal things. She would relate the many special features of having a twin sister, particularly in the growing years. She even laughed about an incident that was quite serious at the time. In high school they were both vying for the affections of the same boy. Cassie could easily relate to the feelings they had at the time, and she would tell her of the romantic adventure with Ethan. Cassie's tears flowed at the final event, and she was sure she would never get used to this no matter how humane it was.

As they walked back to the Inn, James was told of the plan concerning the youngsters. He readily agreed to his part, and even suggested he could work out later developments as over the years he had established a network of people who not only owed him favors but also with their strong beliefs in the right to die were not adverse in participating in actions to help others with different kinds of needs. While they all hoped it would not be needed, it was comforting to know that recourse would be available.

TWENTY-TWO

It was another beautiful spring day. Grady was determined to begin writing the book. After all, the advice Ladson had given him made much sense. You begin by starting it.

He tucked the laptop under his arm and walked to the marsh for further inspiration. There was still an early morning mist hovering over the expanse. He wondered what other secrets were harbored there other than the ones he knew about. The ledge was hard and cold but he was on a mission and barely noticed the discomfort. He opened the laptop and delved into what he knew would be a combination of the real and his imagination. At this point he was not sure how much of each of such components would emerge.

THE MARSH

CHAPTER ONE

Where and how
it all started

Goldsborough, a quaint hamlet in New Hampshire, had been settled mainly by German and Dutch immigrants. It was laid out on a wide strip of land between a river and an expansive marsh area. Because the river had evidently flooded a number of times, there were few trees and fertile soil. It was an ideal place for a colony. Besides farming, a lumber mill was erected to capitalize on the river to transport lumber from the forests to the north and then to the colonies to the south.

Because the marsh was a relatively dark and foreboding place with a variety of thick vegetation, it fostered numerous ominous tales. These were enhanced when Lars Erinkoff went into the marsh after his dog who went in chasing a fox. Lars and the dog never emerged from the marsh. A thorough search by the town folk found nothing. People, particularly children, were told to stay away from the marsh. Thus, it was already shrouded in mystery.

The year was 1693, and the news had just filtered in from Salem in neighboring Massachusetts that 200 young girls after trials had been executed for practicing witchcraft. The superstitious folk of Goldsborough were already on edge because a series of driving rains had destroyed a large portion of the crops. Also, the waterwheel at the mill had unexplainably stopped working and no one could figure out how to get it started again.

Ella Krupoff and Mary Heinreich were rambunctious fourteen year old friends. It seemed as if they were always getting into some kind of trouble. Pent up energy with a constant curiosity are dangerous ingredients for youthful behavior. A jealous playmate thought it would serve them right if she started describing them as witches. That rumor spread through the colony quickly, and when the elders confronted the girls with the accusation shocked silence followed by vehement denial did not help their cause. The parents of the girls adamantly proclaimed the innocence of the girls and labeled the falsehood for what it was, but to no avail as the fearful tide was unstoppable. Without even the semblance of a trial, the girls were to be burned at the stake.

With the help of their parents, the girls escaped the night before they were to be executed. A boat that was supposed to be waiting for them at the river was not there, so in fear and desperation the girls fled to the marsh with only the moonlight to guide them, never to be seen or heard from again. Even to this day, there are folks who swear that on moonlit nights they can hear the wails of anguish coming from the marsh. The secrets of the marsh have never been unlocked.

An eery cry came from the marsh right on cue and he looked up. It sounded as if an animal was being killed. The mist had cleared but he could see nothing. A pervasive silence followed and the tall grasses moved erratically as a breeze swelled up. Satisfied with his efforts as a first draft, Grady headed back to the Inn. After a few steps he stopped and turned around. He did not know exactly what he expected to see. Maybe, it was Ella and Mary. Maybe, it was Lars and his dog. Maybe, it was Lillian, or the Professor, or Doreen and Colleen. Maybe, it was all of them. Seeing nothing he closed his eyes for a moment before continuing his journey.

TWENTY-THREE

Eileen did not have to read Grady's draft chapter to believe that the marsh had some mystical power. How could people just disappear in it? How could it have characteristics which seem to defy the laws of nature? How could it cast a form of spell over those persons who let their mind wander over the how and why of it all?

It was a quiet morning on a beautiful day at the Inn. She completed some chores and told Grady she was going to hike to the marsh. He asked if she wanted him to go with her and she replied she needed to go alone. He tried to reassure her that there was no resident evil there and all of his stories were pure fabrication. Those that entered the marsh for their last moments were probably swallowed up by the muck, akin to quick sand. She told herself that there was probably more to it than that. Eaten by voracious animals was probably more like it, and she was saddened if that were true because it is a ghastly way to die. No, there had to be a hidden kindly spirit that gently guides them to a pastoral place far away. At least that is what she told Cassie when the youngster confronted her with questions about what happened to them. That answer appeared to give Cassie some comfort, but Eileen was not sure about much these days.

Once at the marsh, she leaned on the railing peering in as far as she could. Visually, there were no answers. The longer she stared the more she was inclined to review her own life. In the whirlwind of activities since she met Grady, after her first thought processes there had been little time or incentive for reflection. Now seemed as good a time as any to fully digest where she was and where she was going. The two paramount items were crystal clear. She loved Grady and she loved the Inn. While these two features colored everything else, she did have some doubts and misgivings about other things. While she did not have a religious upbringing, her parents were highly moral and ethical people who constantly briefed her to stay in the right even if there was a fine line between right and wrong. That is why she was so shocked by Grady's original concept for the Inn of removing people. To her, that was an extremely wrong approach. She tried to tell herself that what they were doing for James was far removed from that original scheme. Providing the place and means for people to shorten a suffering existence or a life with little or no quality and meaning while tottering between right and wrong at least in theory leaned more to the right side. Believing this, however, there had to be more humane ways to bring on death than walking into the marsh and being left there to face an uncertain means and timing for that final termination. Yet, the Inn contingency had no actual participation in the death itself. Or was she just rationalizing? Leading a person to a place where the means of death is unknown and beyond control is part of the killing. Is it any better than the final action? James had said on more than one occasion that the basic benefit is that the person has the self-satisfaction of doing it themselves. She was not sure she could ever resolve this as a matter of ethics. There was no escaping that it was all a done deed. This kind of self-debate was probably more appropriate before the first instance.

As for Cassie and Ethan, she had grown to love them as the children she never had. Selfishly, she yearned to hold on to them. Yet, if she were a true parent, and if someone else had secreted them away and without knowing if they were safe and well and with the prospect of never seeing them again, how would she feel? Without them, how could she adjust to all of the mundane facets of day-to-day life? Another instance of a borderline dilemma.

A movement in the marsh interrupted her thoughts. She was not sure what it was but it was gone the instant she saw it. A good thing she was jerked back to actual reality because the more she delved in to things the deeper the quagmire was getting. Then, she saw the movement again. This time she could tell that it was a large bird. As a city person, she was unfamiliar with what it was. It had a large menacing beak and its coloring was captivating. For the lack of anything else, she referred to it as THE WAY IT IS BIRD. The bird captured the essence of her life. This is the way that it is. She started back to her Grady, back to their Inn, back to the now life that she had.

TWENTY-FOUR

It was a week later when Grady went back to the marsh to continue writing the book. He stared intently at the scene before him before turning his attention to the lap top. It was the same marsh, yet in an inexplicable way it looked different than it did the week before. Perhaps it was just the constantly changing spring vegetation. Yet, when he thought about it the marsh never seemed to look the same way twice. There was no way to avoid the sinister conclusion that the marsh was truly alive and menacing. As already proven, its appetite was voracious and nondiscriminatory.

CHAPTER TWO

PRESENT DAY

Goldsborough changed drastically over the centuries. While still small basically because restricted to the same strip of land between the river and the marsh, it was no longer a farming community. The lumber mill too was long since gone. The enclave of old homes captured its quaint descriptive essence, but the nature of its existence and of its residents were totally different. It had become an artists colony. Painters, sculptors, as well as a slew of writers, many traced back to the counter culture of the 1960s, comprised most of the community. Interaction was congenial, and most opened their studios to the tourists that flocked to see their works or to investigate the legend of the marsh. Some converted their homes into bed and breakfast establishments for additional income. The river was used for swimming and other recreational activities, and a host of small boats and canoes were tied up at the docks.

The nature of the marsh had not changed, and its legend was further enhanced by the telling and retelling of the fearful mysteries that lurked in the deep. A walkway had been erected going partway into the marsh so visitors could get a glimpse of the birds and reptiles that frequented the area as well as hopefully be stumped by the tall grasses erratically catching the breezes. Occasionally, an indecipherable sound would emanate from deep within, and hushed comments would affix them as plaintive wails of those lost within. Prominent posted signs warned of the dangers of any other entry into the marsh with a stiff penalty for those who did. Many of the artists had works depicting the gloom of the marsh for those who wanted or needed a reminder of the excursion.

One set of artist owners, Brady and Irene Winslow, had a house closest to the marsh, and especially on moonlit nights a distant cry in the marsh would wake them up. They had been students at the University of California, Berkeley, in the 1960s and active protestors against the war in Vietnam and other dictates of a staid society. Brady was a student leader and Irene a flower child who roamed Haight-Asbury singing and dancing with the throng of free spirits. They knew one another but were too involved in their surroundings to spend time together. After graduation, they met again at a painting class and started dating. Both had not fully settled down and even now shades of their liberal past would emerge in politics or in battles with local causes. They did not believe in marriage but married solely for Brady to be deferred from the draft. Their painting styles were similar except Brady used broader brush strokes. They had heard about a new commune starting in

Vermont, so they drove their old car cross-country only to find out that there was no such commune. A local merchant had just bought a painting from an artist who told him about Goldsborough, New Hampshire. That is where they went and have been ever since. Between the river, the marsh, and the surrounding countryside, there was plenty to paint. The marsh was a new experience, almost psychedelic. Each painting they did of that foreboding place they would attach a story to it. Each season brought forth new spectacles to be captured, new entrapments for the imagination.

They had much in common with their neighbors so there was easy and enjoyable socialization, intellectual commentary running freely. Since the house they had bought for a very low price was large, they converted it into a bed and breakfast as others were doing. Tourists were plenty except in the winter when they had the place all to themselves. The tourists liked them because they were friendly and talkative, and children especially hung on all of their embellished stories about the marsh.

Never ones to shun radical ideas, a casual remark by a neighbor that there was a potential for other things in the marsh, clandestine things, led them to think long and hard in that direction. In the middle of the night, Irene shook Brady awake, shouting at him in almost a shriek, "It can be used to dispose of bodies!"

TWENTY-FIVE

Eileen read the second chapter and stroked Grady's cheek. "You sure do make it all sound intriguing. I like the Brady and Irene fix. Yet, at some point, might it be interpreted as a confession of sorts?"

"Might be. Also, might be a catharsis. At this juncture I am not sure how much more I will write. It is stimulating in one way, draining in another. Whether I finish it or not, you will probably be the only one to read it."

"A wifely privilege. Clever, too. A wife can't testify against her husband I read somewhere or saw on television years ago."

"It's a spousal privilege. I can't testify against you either."

Eileen chuckled. "Ah! So others might point fingers of guilt at us but we can't condemn each other."

They were interrupted by the arrival of James with the next guest to find endless time. Arnold Coogan was a ninety-one year old invalid. The collapsible wheelchair was in the trunk of the car. Arnold's full head of thick gray hair and ruddy cheeks did not define his declining condition. James had picked him up directly from the nursing home where his inconsiderate children had placed him more than ten years earlier. There, he was further withering away.

Ethan helped him out of the car and into the wheelchair. Cassie pushed the chair to the room he would be occupying and Ethan followed with a small satchel. Cassie unpacked the few things that were in the bag, talking to Arnold the entire time as if they were old friends. Arnold said nothing in return but he soaked in every word the young woman uttered. It was not until she wheeled him to the dining room for lunch did he speak to her. To her surprise, his voice was deep and full defying his otherwise frail body. "Please keep me company while I eat. Then, I would like you to take me to the marsh."

Cassie smiled, patted his hand and sat next to where she pushed the wheelchair to the table. "It will be a bumpy ride. Are you up to it?"

With a touch of humor which was a surprise to him as well as to her, he said lightly, "I better be."

She went to the kitchen and came out with a plate for him as well as for herself. Between mouth fulls, Cassie detailed the attributes of the Inn and described her life there with Ethan. Through it all Arnold was quiet and pensive. He picked at the food as his appetite was nearly nonexistent.

When they arrived at the marsh, Arnold stared out to the spectacle before him through the thick lenses of his glasses. He knew he had come to a place that would welcome him. Cassie sat on the ledge next to him, and for the first time in a long period he actually wanted to talk. "I appreciate your attention and telling me about your life here. I can understand the draw that it has. I have some advice for you. But, first, I want to tell you about my life so that the lesson I let you in on will be more meaningful. I will spare you the details as that way I will not have to relive them. The details are also unimportant for the message." The full voice turned raspy and Cassie strained to hear his every word. She was going to tell him to spare himself if he was in pain, but he continued before she could say anything. "To this day, I still do not know if life is better if you have choices or no choices. Some people, either because of economics or other circumstances, have no real choice what to do with their lives. A job, a neighborhood, and who they associate with are limited options. Yet, they can reach a certain contentment if they accept things as they are. Those that have a range of choices can be frustrated because they are unsure whether they made the right decision or because other options become enticing. I was restless as a boy. My parents were well off and gave me everything I could possibly want. I know I would have been a better person if only then they had given me just what I needed. The capacity to be satisfied was lost. I graduated from law school not because I wanted to be a lawyer. I believed that having a law degree would enhance my appeal and value in the business world. It did that, but beyond each undertaking I perceived a greater challenge elsewhere so that I went from job to job with no lasting satisfaction in what I was doing. Marriage and family was the same story. My first marriage was to a woman whose only interests were the home and the two children we had. I found her to be dull and boring. My participation in matters relating to the home and the children were minimal and unenthusiastic. I welcomed her overture for a divorce and she and the children had little to do with me after that. My second marriage was to a career woman, and that did not last long. She had the attitude that her business skills were in competition with mine, and there was constant friction. Through all of my business activities and domestic situations I was basically a lonely man. After the second divorce, that loneliness became oppressive. I had comforts and independence but that sort of happiness, if it is even happiness, was short lived. My life was doomed. My health and physical condition declined to the point where I could no longer work or take care of myself. The ex-wives, even if they might have done something caring, had predeceased me. The adult children would not take me in, and I suppose out of some distant obligation they collectively put me in a nursing home and then totally forgot me. So, there I languished until James convinced me that I had one more choice." Arnold fell silent.

Cassie stood and leaned over to hug him. She clasped a weak hand and said gently, "That is not your only choice. You can stay here with me in this beautiful and peaceful place. I will take care of you. I will keep you company. I will make sure you have some happiness."

Arnold put his other hand on top of her hand. "You are a sweet and kind person. I have finally learned the difference between a choice and a wish, I may wish to be here with you, but death is the real choice. It is my clear end to a cloudy life."

Cassie was crying so hard she could not speak. Arnold continued talking, his voice now displaying the urgency to impart what he wanted to say while he still could. "Here is the lesson you need to learn from me. I can tell you and Ethan love each other. Love is the beginning and not the end. You need to grow together or you will grow apart. Do as much for him as you can, and be appreciative of all he does for you. Be pleasant and courteous with one another. Even in a disagreement be respectful of another opinion. Share the fruits of your love with others. Make your small world benevolent even if the larger world is hostile."

Cassie dabbed her eyes with a tissue and realized Arnold had fallen asleep. She left her hand in his and continued crying. As if the marsh had witnessed it all, a slight breeze came from within and caressed her cheek.

TWENTY-SIX

The next morning, Grady and Ethan carried Arnold into the marsh while James and tearful Cassie looked on from the railing. Ethan was trembling, and he knew it was not from the wet and cold spilling into his boots and clinging to his jeans. He had not been this close to death before, and once inside the marsh it was truly intimidating. Centuries of hidden secrets surrounded him and consumed his thoughts.

Back in their room, Cassie could tell that Ethan was troubled. "What is it, sweets?"

Ethan held her close. "I am not sure if it is the marsh or death, or both, that haunts me. Rubbing elbows with death is probably the last thing young people experience."

Cassie returned his embrace with earnest strength. "Yes, but it is part of our life here now. I'll never like it although I try to make sense out of it. On the plus side, we have not been exposed to old people before except for Ladson. Their experience gives them much wisdom, and if we listen carefully to them there is a great deal we can learn. I told you last night about what Arnold's lesson for us was. That is just a sample of that kind of reason. I like to think our love instinctively knows what he offered, but it is certainly thought-provoking to hear it expressed from one who has been there."

"We should try to learn as much as we can from the people who pass through here. But, I can't escape the conclusion that death is so final."

"I can see it now that it was absurd for us to even consider suicide at one point. It is not a solution for anything."

"Yes, but there is no denying these folks are committing suicide."

"I don't see it that way. And if it is, it is for a noble purpose."

"Perhaps, we should not scrutinize it so closely."

"I have talked to Eileen several times about all of this. She is troubled by it but says that at times what may not seem to make sense in the abstract takes on a different interpretation when you are part of it. She accepts it is an act of mercy. Maybe, it is a question of semantics, but as long as we are here carrying out the purpose of our Inn family's design makes it our purpose as well. Our loyalty must be as firm as that of Cuba and Hilda."

"I suppose in some crucial ways we are no longer young. What we have been exposed to is a maturing trip."

They showered together. All of the vestiges of mud were washed from Ethan's body and in a way from his mind as well. The marsh was not evil in its own right. It was merely a tool for carrying out the expectancies of those who sought its power. They then went to the kitchen to help out. Their togetherness would be the life to Arnold's words even though he was gone.

TWENTY-SEVEN

It was three months before James brought another individual to exercise the final right. The major development during that period was that both Cassie and Ethan celebrated their eighteenth birthdays, which were coincidentally eighteen days apart. Hilda's fancy birthday cakes were consumed with milk and gusto. It also prompted another kitchen meeting.

Sitting around the kitchen work table, an airing of their community wisdom was on the agenda. Family reason was sought from family love.

Grady opened the meeting with the gist of the problem. "We are now all adults." He smiled. "Let me rephrase that. We are now four married adults and two unmarried adults. The obvious, but maybe not the best change, would be for all to be married. As I see it, if the two of you want to get married, the act of filing for a license and the taking of the blood test will be matters of public record and then it will be easy for anyone to track you down here."

Ethan spoke up quickly. "Cass and I have already discussed this. Sure, we would like to be married, but we consider ourselves already married. We don't think it is worth the risk for our being discovered here, not for us since we are of age and can do what we want, but it will put you all and the Inn at risk. I can't say for sure if the parents will be vindictive, but a clever lawyer could probably hatch up a bunch of theories to make your lives miserable. If the police enter the picture, things can get ugly."

"You both keep on demonstrating traits that reinforce our

love for you," Eileen said tearfully, "But your happiness overrides what we may face."

Cassie chimed right in. "We couldn't be happier than we are right now. An actual marriage will come eventually, but as my sweets said we are already married in the sense that our hearts and souls are intertwined."

"I certainly can relate to that," Eileen offered. "I feel that way with Grady, although it was nice to be married, especially here at the Inn."

Ethan spoke up again. "We will just let things go on as they are for now, and the future will hold its promise in that future."

"I have an idea," Cuba interjected, "Why don't we have a wedding anyway? I'll make a feast just as I did when Grady and Eileen tied the knot."

"And I will make another Endless Inn wedding cake," Hilda pronounced.

"Great idea," Grady shouted. "All in favor raise your hand."

Everybody raised two hands. Cassie and Ethan kissed to seal the deal.

Three days later, Cassie and Ethan read aloud together the vow that Grady had penned for the occasion. For a change, there were tears of joy.

At this moment, on this spot, we declare our immense
love for one another for now and for endless time.
Our now and forever family bear witness to this
eternal pact which is irrefutable and unbreakable.

The feast followed. The two guests that were staying in the Inn at the time probably thought there was a drunken horde in the kitchen. Cheers and laughter filled the Inn. The special bottle of wine that Grady opened was just the right accompaniment to Cuba's wedding roast. The scrumptious wedding cake lasted for four days, prolonging the meaningful celebration. Even the marsh could not detract from this special event.

TWENTY-EIGHT

When Mimi Henderson stepped out of the car with James looking on, her frail legs could barely support her but that could not detract from the sense of majesty taking hold. The beauty of the place enthralled her. Living her entire life in a city where she taught English in a high school for nearly forty years, this essence of the country swept her mind away. Then, when the young woman hugged her so warmly, for a moment Mimi thought she had already died and was in Heaven.

At age sixty-three, Mimi had already undergone three surgeries since her first heart attack. She had enough of desperate measures to try and ward off death. She refused to have another operation and was now impatient for the final moment. Death would be a release from the anguish. Her impatience led her to James to hasten the time. It was bad enough through this that she had to give up teaching, and as long as she had any strength her will and determination would let her keep on writing poetry which was her true love in an otherwise loveless life.

Mimi was immediately taken and absorbed in Cassie's overt caring qualities, qualities she knew human beings were capable of but which she had rarely seen firsthand. That alone had her prolong the venture into the marsh for a week. The additional elements of nature and the wonderful food were refreshing for her tired being.

"I suppose I have no regrets," she said to Cassie with some melancholy, "Not that it would do any good to have them, but no man ever proposed to me, although I probably would have turned him down since I was unable to have children. My students were my children, and so many have gone on to lead exemplary lives I know I was a good teacher and in most cases a parent as well. I wonder if I could have done even better if I was perceptive enough to know all those who needed the kind of special touch you have. That you have bestowed that special touch on me, I am so very grateful. I thank you from the bottom of my heart."

"It is I who should thank you," Cassie said slowly. "I have enjoyed our walks and time together. Your stories have been inspiring. I love people, love helping them. I love you. I only wish I could do more to ease the way for you."

"My dear, Cassie, you have done that. I have made my decision because it is right for me. I see that even clearer now because you have given me some final happy moments."

Before Grady led Mimi into the marsh, Mimi handed Cassie a folded piece of paper. Cassie did not open it until later when they had returned to the Inn.

As a final act of the way I love best, I have written this poem for you.

Mimi

THE LADY OF ENDLESS TIME

There is a special lady and Cassie is her name,
Her kind acts while small in scope
Give all that is required for fame,
Gentle kindness is itself hope.

I leave behind a life unglamorous,
Hopefully, I have steered some well;
Even my poems will not make me famous,

But I have one final story to tell.
Cassie is the light to pierce the dark,
For those in need of a genuine design;
A gentle loving support for those ready to embark,
Cassie is the story for all time.

Cassie clutched the poem to her heart and cried again as she had at the railing as Grady and Mimi disappeared from view. She would cherish it and the memory of Mimi until her own final breath.

TWENTY-NINE

Grady wrestled with himself repeatedly about the book. He was busy enough with the Inn, and he preferred spending any spare time with Eileen. Walking together or reading in the book nook were favorite pastimes. Writing is, after all, such a solitary exercise. An author delights and suffers alone. Yet, writing can be a forceful compulsion. He eventually decided that he would write one more chapter before resolving the dilemma.

It was a windy fall day, and even the sun did little to diminish the chill. Several times on the way to the marsh he was tempted to turn back. Once at the marsh it appeared as if every part of that enigma was in motion. Perhaps, it was digesting bodies. If that did not put him in the mood for writing, nothing would.

CHAPTER THREE

A PLAN CONCEIVED

"Disposing of bodies!" Brady's shout echoed Irene's outburst. "Are you serious? What do you mean exactly?"

Irene was thoughtful for a moment. "Gee, I'm not sure. But, I figure if I had a body and wanted it gone, I'd pay big bucks to someone who could get rid of it."

"Probably so. Yet, how would you know who has a body? If it was from a criminal act, that would mean you are an accessory, a criminal act, too. Also, if it was a criminal, he or she might make it two bodies."

"How so?"

"To guarantee it is kept secret, you dispense with the dispenser."

"Oh! O.K., then who else would want a body gone that they did not kill?"

"Beats me. If a person died legally, then it could just be buried or cremated legally."

"I guess it was too good to be true."

"Not necessarily."

"What are you driving at?"

"What if it is not a dead body?"

"Someone alive, you mean?"

"Yup."

"How? Where?"

"What if someone wanted to commit suicide and not be found or found out?"

"Who would walk into a marsh to die when they could just take a pill or something like that?"

"Again, if they did not want to be found. Insurance policies don't pay off for suicides. If there is no body, seems to me they can't prove a suicide?"

"How then do they establish the person insured has died?"

"I'm not sure, but there are probably ways. After a period of time someone is probably assumed dead."

"How do you know who would want to do that?"

"That's where you have to be clever. You concoct a story about someone coming to the marsh to end his life there. The community tries to talk him out of it but he does it anyway. The police are called in and a search finds nothing. You spice it up so that the story is picked up as national coverage. Then you sit back and wait for just the right people who put two and two together."

Irene was quiet for a moment. "Why would they pay us for doing this. They could just walk in on their own. Signs telling them they can't won't stop them."

"Incentive and frills. You offer them something appealing first, like a vacation or granting a last wish, and then a guide to take them to the right place to maximize results."

"It's starting to sound awfully gruesome. I'm sorry I said anything."

"Don't be sorry. It was a stroke of genius. You had the idea, and I am mean enough and greedy enough to carry it through.

Let's just hope it pays as well as I hope. Anyway, let's sleep on it."

"Who can sleep?"

THIRTY

Eileen answered the telephone when James called. She noticed it had just started to snow and she thought that indicated they would be in for another harsh winter. Winter was not a time to sojourn into the marsh. All that ice and frigid temperatures would be extra hard on the person as well as for Ethan. At Ethan's request, Grady had agreed to let him be the escort into the marsh from now on. It was becoming physically demanding, and Grady had to admit since he had become an emotional softie it was a tough mind set too. He did not think he could turn his back on another person facing that kind of death alone.

"I know it is not the best time," James began, "But I have a desperate situation. Bennie and Esther Arnett are in their late eighties. They have been married for sixty-four years and have no children or other living relatives. They have an array of infirmities but are not facing a terminal situation as far as I know. They have been in a nursing home for seven years. To get in they had to sign over all of their assets. That nursing home is now closing and they have no place to go to. All the State run facilities are already overcrowded. At this point, they have contacted me and just want to die together. I have explained the hardship and discomfort at this time of year, but they are adamant. As my heart breaks for them, I will pay the cost. I will understand if you turn this one down, I'll just have to find another alternative."

When Eileen was sure he had finished, she said thoughtfully, "I just don't know offhand. I need to talk to Grady, and we'll call you later."

Eileen assembled Grady, Cassie, and Ethan in the book nook, and explained the situation to them. As expected, Cassie started crying and managed to utter her usual heart-generated thoughts. "Can't we just care for them at least until spring?"

Grady responded as best he could. "James will pay for a few days, but we can't just give up a room for a long period of time. It will hurt financially."

Cassie blurted out between sobs, "Ethan and I will give up our room."

Ethan put his arm around her shoulders. "We can sleep on cots in the kitchen."

Eileen hugged them both. "Just what I should have expected you'd say. I don't want to seem uncaring about this and cold as I feel sorry for these people too, but it is unrealistic for us to care for them. We are not trained in such care, and they undoubtedly would have needs we cannot tend to."

"All well and good," Cassie said softly. "But we can try."

Grady tried to sum it all up. "So, we will tell James to try and make other arrangements and if he can't we'll keep them here until spring at our expense."

"You know as well as I do," Eileen interjected, "That he will pounce on this and not even try elsewhere."

"So be it," Grady philosophized.

"And so it shall be done," Eileen said as she hugged Cassie. "We will not, however, let you sleep in the kitchen. The winter looks like it will be bad so we probably won't be full all of the time. If by some chance we are, we will set up the cots in our room."

"We don't want to infringe on your privacy," Ethan offered.

"I hope you know by now," Eileen put her hand on his arm, "Family love can be as powerful as the love you two share."

"I am learning that daily," Ethan responded. "Forgive me that it just takes some time to accept."

Grady spoke up pensively, "I remember a sign I saw some years back. It sums up our situation:

We may not have it all together
But together we have it all."

That night locked in their usual loving embrace, Grady said softly in Eileen's ear, "I sure am one lucky guy. I lucked out with you; I lucked out with Cuba and Hilda; and I certainly lucked out with Cassie and Ethan."

"Yes, we did luck out with them. They are wonderful youngsters and I love them as if they were our own children."

"Me, too."

"I dread the day they leave us."

"That might never happen. Even if they eventually do leave us, I know we will not lose them."

THIRTY-ONE

The new arrivals were far less trouble than anticipated. They were quiet and made no demands. Cassie was their nearly constant companion, and it was evident from the start there was a mutual love relationship. They also did not eat much which partially would account for their frail condition. For breakfast and lunch Cassie would bring a tray to their room which had small portions of the fare offered. She would bring them to the dining room for dinner, and Cassie and Ethan would bring them meals from the kitchen and would dine with them. Each day they opened up a little bit more, and with the relaxed atmosphere they became more talkative. There was obvious joy in talking about their earlier lives.

Bennie had been an appliance salesman most of his adult life, but he liked mostly to talk about the array of jobs he had when he was younger. Since he was small in stature, for a time he was a jockey. He exclaimed that was a thrill a minute, even if he never rode a winning horse. Then, he was a caddy at a country club and had a glimpse of how the other half live. The hardest job he ever had was as a pin boy at a bowling alley. In the days before that sort of operation was automated, the pins had to be gathered manually from wherever they landed and set in racks that were lowered by hand for the pins to be set up. If one wobbled enough to fall over, the whole thing had to be done over. He usually worked four adjoining alleys, and the balls and pins would scatter all over, some with great force when a strong bowler let a ball fly. He had to keep moving constantly from alley to alley all the time watching for flying pins, which were quite heavy. Players would throw coins down the alley for a tip, and that meant keeping track of the games.

Bennie met Esther when he was working the soda fountain at a drug store. She was a seamstress at a garment factory near by and twice a week she stopped by with two of her friends at the soda fountain for a soda. Bennie did not care about the thick lenses in her glasses caused by the poor eyesight from the strain at the factory over time and with poor lighting conditions. He just accepted that it made her beautiful blue eyes look bigger. Since he did not meet many girls that were shorter than him, that was also an initial attraction. She would linger at the fountain after her friends left, and their conversations became longer and more personal. They discovered they had much in common, especially ideas and dreams. After dating for several months they eloped and a long and loving life began. Even after finding out that Esther could not have children that did not daunt their moments together. They loved to go to the movies and listen to classical music on the radio. Because of her poor eyesight she could not drive and was not able to work full time. She had an assortment of part time jobs, most often in sales for the Christmas season. On vacations, they went on bus tours to an array of tourist spots and took many pictures as the technology of cameras steadily improved. They let Cassie look through the albums containing the photographs.

They did not have kind remarks about the period they were in the nursing home. They had to sign over all of their assets just to get in, and the treatment there was below par. The staff was not adequate or trained enough to take care of the residents. Some of the people there were unkind to them, perhaps being envious of their togetherness. One bitter woman shouted at them in front of many of the others, "What do you have to show for all of the years you have existed?" They knew better than to say anything as it would just incite the woman to more ranting. Such a remark was hurtful but they were secure in the fact they had shared their own adventures. While their accomplishments were not socially noteworthy and even petty in the eyes of others, they knew what was really important was that they had made a life together totally their own. That was the vital lesson they impressed on Cassie. You do not live your life for others. You live it for yourself.

Two months later the winter abated. On an initial warm day, the old folks asked Cassie to take them to the marsh. They had heard so much about it, they wanted to see it for themselves.

It took awhile for the hike to be completed, and once there Bennie and Esther sat on the ledge taking in the vista. Esther's eyes probably did not allow her to see much, but Bennie described it all to her.

"It is not as intimidating as I thought it would be," Bennie spoke after awhile. Another gift of old age, as Cassie was learning, is that older people can often see beauty where others might only see anguish.

"Well, you can admire it any way you want," Cassie said sternly," Because this is as close to it as you are going to get."

"And we see the beauty in you," Esther added.

It was nearly dark by the time they returned to the Inn. They asked Cassie to just bring them light food and hot tea as they were too tired to go to the dining room.

The next day was also beautiful, and even early in the morning the sun captured a renewed warmth. As usual, Cassie emerged from the kitchen with a tray for her special charges. There was no response when she knocked on the door. She thought they might still be asleep after the exhausting day before. She tried the door and it was unlocked. Upon entering, it was obvious that the bed was still as she had made it up the day before. They had not slept there. The tears welled up in Cassie's eyes as she suspected the worst. She placed the tray on the table and looked around carefully. The albums were there but all of the photographs had been removed. There was an envelope on the dresser that had her name on it.

She opened it, and read it slowly through the flowing tears.

Dear Cassie and the rest of the caring Inn people:

Words are inadequate to express the peace and contentment we had here these months. We thank you deeply for the love and caring we received.

You have done enough for us. We give you back the room so that there may not be further losses for you.

It is time for us to do something for you. It is also time for our final journey while we are still able to be together. Our final wish for all of you is for long lives filled with success and happiness. Continue as you are.

With love -
Bennie and Esther

Cassie shouted out for Ethan, and the two ran all the way to the marsh. Cassie was crying the entire time, and the tears flowed even more when they found nothing at the marsh. There was not a sign that anyone had been there. Ethan ventured part way into the marsh only to return shortly with head bowed low. Bennie and Esther were gone. Cassie hoped that her tears would help carry them gently to their final destination.

THIRTY-TWO

Six weeks later a special celebration was held at the Inn to mark Grady's seventieth birthday. A joint effort in the kitchen by Cuba, Hilda, Cassie, and Ethan produced a feast befitting a king. Eileen gave him a personal gift of the initial sketches she had made of the book nook, the dining room, and other areas all framed and ready to hang in the entrance way. It was a memorable time by all accounts.

The next day Grady hiked to the marsh. He needed to be alone with his thoughts, a rarity for him. He did not feel old, but there comes a time in the progression of life when one should devise a stopping place to review that life.

What emerged first in the introspection was the conjecture about all of those years of sacrifice for an enterprise that did not come into fruition. Was it all for nothing? That might be a fast and easy conclusion. Yet, if he stepped back and scrutinized all that had happened since his retirement, it made up for everything that preceded it and then some. Without the sacrifices, he would not have had the money to buy the Inn and start it as a business. He was comfortable with and liked the whole aspect of innkeeping, including tending to the grounds and trails which was an activity he had prepared himself for throughout the years. The Inn being successful was an essential part of his dreams. Without the Inn, he would not have been able to entice the superior culinary couple, Cuba and Hilda, to perform the vital part of the business of gourmet meals. Further, he would not have the security of their friendship and loyalty. Without the Inn, he would never have met Eileen and discovered his capacity to love and reap the benefits of being loved by such an extraordinary woman. Without the Inn and its fortuitous nature and design to be able to hide persons who need to escape from dire situations, he would never have experienced the form and content of family love when Cassie and Ethan entered his life and filled a void he did not realize existed until then. It had been a major relief for all of them when Ladson finally realized that the parents were merely feigning concern for the youngsters by hiring a private detective. The sobering situation probably was paramount that since the couple was now of legal age, parental options were restricted. Perhaps, they were even subdued by actually not having to get involved in a situation that was beyond their control. The likelihood now was that the loving couple would remain at the Inn. Grady's early sense of a need to do something important had over time taken the form of facilitating certain people in their quest of the right to die, a right that he had come to learn was a powerful driving force. He was in this respect doing something good for others as well as himself. His decision about giving up on any further writing of the book was, at least for now, the best decision. Selfishly, this way he would not be distracted from the other facets of his life. He would not completely rule out continuing on it in the future.

He stared out over the marsh astounded that a feature of nature could be so much a part of his being. As if his thoughts were being spoken aloud and being answered, a brisk wind came up blowing the tall grasses in various directions. The marsh was not only alive, it could actually express itself. He might not ever fully understand all of its variations and vagaries, but he would always respect it. It was the epitome of endless time.

www.ingramcontent.com/pod-product-compliance
Ingram Content Group UK Ltd.
Pitfield, Milton Keynes, MK11 3LW, UK
UKHW041852190726
13854UKWH00002B/866